HEART OF STONE

She would never forget this night

Travelling to Scandinavia to manage the Sornefjord Hotel, Kessie Danton is shocked by the instant antipathy between herself and the owner's son, Brent Tolkelarson. A sojourn sheltering from a blizzard inside a mountain hut seems to clear up some of their differences, but brings to light a powerful attraction that threatens to make life even more awkward.

HEART OF STONE

HEART OF STONE

Iris Gower

Severn House Large Print
London & New York

This first large print edition published in Great Britain 2002 by
SEVERN HOUSE LARGE PRINT BOOKS LTD of
9-15, High Street, Sutton, Surrey, SM1 1DF.
First regular print edition published 2001 by
Severn House Publishers, London and New York.
This first large print edition published in the USA 2002 by
SEVERN HOUSE PUBLISHERS INC., of
595 Madison Avenue, New York, NY 10022

British Library Cataloguing in Publication Data

Gower, Iris
  Heart of stone - Large pr
  1. Love stories
  2. Large type books
  I. Title II. That sweet a
  823.9'14 [F]

  ISBN 0-7278-7148-X

Except where actual historica
described for the storyline of
publication are fictitious and any resemblance to living persons is
purely coincidental.

Printed and bound in Great Britain by
MPG Books Ltd, Bodmin, Cornwall.

ONE

Kessie took a deep breath of the crisp mountain air, allowing the reins to go slack in her fingers as the animal beneath her strained up the steep slope, head plunging forward, shoes ringing against the shower of loose stones. The plateau rose above the riders, magnificent, iced with the white snow on the top crevices. It seemed that they would never reach it.

Kessie glanced at the man beside her. He was as stony as any mountain, his face set, his head high as he skilfully directed his horse over the uneven ground. And yet she sensed fire beneath the cold exterior.

"Do you resent my coming here?" she asked, speaking in her more than adequate

Norwegian. He answered her in excellent English.

"Why should I?"

Embarrassed by his brevity, she rushed on. "Your father has been so kind to me." Her words almost tripped from her tongue, her agitation showing in the trembling of her hands. "I don't know what I'd have done if Lars hadn't offered me a position here as manageress of his new hotel. I was so happy to come to Norway."

"I have no interest in your problems, Miss Danton." His voice was as cold as the snow on the hills. "I only have the interest of my father at heart."

Even in her distress, Kessie couldn't help admiring the precise English and the resonant tones of Brent's voice.

"I am concerned with your father's interests, too," she said quickly. "I am very fond of Lars, he was so good to me when my own father died. Why, he even bought the Danton from me, knowing I couldn't afford to run the place myself, I simply didn't have the resources."

"Ah yes, the Danton." Brent looked away up into the mountain and Kessie tried to read by his tone of voice just what he was thinking.

"Well, what about the Danton?" she demanded and he looked across at her, an ironic smile twisting his mouth.

"I shouldn't think I'd need to say anything at all about that subject, Miss Danton, since you should know better than I what the true worth of the place is."

They looked at each other for a moment in silence and Kessie saw how the sun brought out the gold of his hair so that the smooth skin of his face seemed brown in comparison with those strange grey eyes, Brent was a very handsome, compelling man.

He spurred his animal forward, riding a little way ahead of Kessie. His muscles rippled beneath the taut material of his jacket as he handled the spirited horse with the ease of long practice. She forced herself to look away from him.

"Why didn't someone think of letting me

know that the hotel was inaccessible on foot?" Kessie said, feeling the strain of the unaccustomed mode of travel. She hadn't ridden a horse since she was a child and even then she'd never been very good.

Brent glanced back at her. "Would it have made any difference? In any case, it's only inaccessible when we've had a fall of snow." He gave a wry smile, "Of course that's something that happens quite frequently here in Norway, I must admit."

She looked at him, meeting his eyes for a brief second before looking away. Brent glanced at his watch.

"We don't seem to be making very good time, not much of a rider, are you?"

She ignored his remark, pressing her lips together, trying to push aside the anger and the overwhelming sense of tiredness she was feeling. She'd had a long journey and could well do without the undoubted hostility Brent was directing towards her.

"About my luggage," she said after a while, "when will it be brought up from the valley?"

He smiled. "There's plenty of time for that, after all you might decide not to stay when you see how solitary the hotel is."

Kessie looked up and saw that a blue shading of cloud had obscured the top of the mountain. The night was drawing in quickly and she shivered.

"Would you like to stop and get a coat from your saddle bag?" Brent spoke politely, and yet there was a hint of laughter in his voice as though he thought she was some sort of city weakling.

"I'm all right," she said abruptly. "Are we nearly there yet?"

"No." The word was flat. "We should be but don't blame yourself." His tone implied she was precisely the one to blame.

Kessie rode on, aware that the air was getting colder. It would have been sensible to put on a coat, though when they'd begun to ride from the base of the mountain it had been warm and sunny, so pleasant that it had seemed almost summer instead of early spring.

She glanced up at the sky. It was darkening even as she watched, great clouds rolled overhead, threatening to swirl down upon her any moment.

"Come," Brent's voice was terse. "Keep close behind me, I would not like you to get lost." He swung his horse away from the well rutted track on to the grass. Above them, the plateau had disappeared and a keen wind was blowing into Kessie's face, lifting her dark red hair away from her shoulders.

A bird suddenly swooped downwards, frightening the animal Kessie was riding. The horse reared suddenly and the ground swung away from Kessie. She felt herself falling and there was nothing she could do to save herself. She hit the ground hard and rolled over several times, coming to rest breathless and shaken against a soft grass bank.

Brent was at her side immediately. "Are you all right?" He lifted her bodily and she was aware of the sheer brute strength of him as he held her as easily as though she'd been a child.

In the distance, she could see the startled horse bolting, mane flying in the wind, legs stretched for speed in spite of the ruggedness of the terrain.

"Oh, I'm sorry!" she said as the full realisation of what had happened hit her. He set her gently on her feet.

"Can you stand?" Brent said, his face inscrutable; and she nodded, wincing a little as she put her full weight on her ankle, only then feeling the pain.

"I think I've sprained my ankle," she admitted in a low voice.

Brent took her in his arms once more, lifting her into the saddle of his own horse. She was acutely aware of the fragrant smell of his skin and the warmth of his hands as they held her, though Kessie pushed aside the thought that she was attracted to this man.

"I hope your managing capabilities are more promising than your horsemanship," Brent said without a trace of a smile, and Kessie felt absurd tears spring to her eyes. He was determined to be unpleasant to her, though for the life of her she couldn't

13

understand why.

"I don't have to account to you on that score," Kessie said tersely. "I think your father has every confidence in me, so I should mind my own business if I were you!"

As soon as she uttered the words, she felt as though she'd been childish. She turned her face down into the thin collar of her jacket trying to shield herself from the cutting hail that had begun to fall.

"We shall have to find shelter," Brent said, ignoring her remarks as though he hadn't heard them. "We won't be able to see a yard in front of us if this keeps up."

"Shelter?" Kessie's voice rose. "Where on earth can we find shelter on this barren mountainside?"

"That, as you would say, Miss Danton, is my business." Brent almost smiled and Kessie fell into a silence that was as deep and uncomfortable as the snow now forming around her hair and eyelashes.

He led the horse forward, walking carefully, his head thrown back. Kessie wondered how he could see anything at all because she could hardly keep her eyes open.

"Here we are," Brent said, and Kessie, peering through the gloom, was just able to make out a dark shape against the blizzard.

"Come along." His hands were lifting her from the saddle, and impatiently Kessie pushed him away, with the result that she slipped and fell heavily into the coldness of the snow.

Without a word, Brent hauled her up into his arms and kicking open the door of what looked like a mere hut, took her inside.

She sat and watched as he led the horse to the far end of the hut, her eyes were wide and Brent gave her an amused glance.

"Never shared a room with a horse before, have you?" he said, and she shook her head emphatically.

"No, and I don't particularly want to do so right now but it seems I've no choice."

"You'll be pleased this animal is here," Brent said, opening one of the saddle bags, "because here I have the means of lighting us a fire. That could be a factor in saving our lives, do you understand?"

Kessie stared at him. "Are things that bad?" she asked. "Surely Lars will send someone out to find us when we don't turn up at the hotel on time?"

He sighed, obviously exasperated at her stupidity. "No one can ride in this storm. In any case, my father knows that I have enough sense to find us shelter. When the storm dies down, a search party will be organised, just to be on the safe side."

"How long do these storms usually last?" Kessie was shivering now. The snow on her clothes had turned to water and she was slowly becoming very wet.

He shrugged. "One, two days, perhaps more." He crouched down before a rough fireplace. "We might as well make ourselves comfortable, don't you agree?"

Kessie had the feeling that Brent was deliberately trying to alarm her and so she remained silent, watching him as he took some wood from the pile in the corner and began to set a fire. It certainly would cheer up the spartan conditions in the small hut.

Kessie looked around her. There were no furnishings as such, just a bunk set against the wall and a cupboard of rough wood standing to the side of the fireplace.

"Well, make yourself useful." Brent's voice startled her and she stared at him questioningly. "Make us some coffee, you are capable of doing that much, aren't you?"

In these primitive surroundings Kessie was not confident of anything, but she got to her feet and looked round her for a moment before crossing to the cupboard.

Inside, there were several tins of meat, and eventually Kessie discovered the coffee.

"Where do I get water?" she asked, and Brent looked up from the fire, his face warmed by the glow, his grey eyes dancing with lights so that he looked almost devilish.

"Out there, my dear girl." He pointed to the door. "Snow turns to water, or haven't you noticed?"

"All right!" she said furiously. "Be sarcastic, but I'd like to see how you would manage if you were taken out of your own environment."

As she limped across towards the door, Kessie had the uncomfortable feeling that Brent was laughing at her. She had no doubt that he would never be at a loss whatever his surroundings.

The force of the wind almost knocked her off her feet. Kessie quickly scooped up some snow into the iron pot and closed the door with a sigh of relief. She could quite see that no search party could venture out in such conditions.

As Kessie placed the pot on the flames, Brent leaned forward and caught the collar of her jacket in his hand.

"You'd better take it off," he said, "otherwise you'll probably get a cold, it's soaking." His tone said that she had no more sense than she was born with and Kessie felt herself colour up. Nevertheless, she took off her jacket and spread it before the fire.

"Your trousers, too," he said pointing, "look, they are clinging to your legs."

"No." Kessie shook her head, she couldn't imagine sitting, wearing only her underclothes, in the same confined quarters as a man like Brent Tolkelarson.

He half smiled as though reading her thoughts, "It's quite all right," he said, "I have no intention of forcing myself on you, you'll be safe in that respect."

His words stung and she turned away from him, seating herself on the bunk, trying to ignore the pain in her ankle and the discomfort of her wet trousers.

He got to his feet and came across to the bunk and Kessie stared up at him as he bent down and fished beneath the bunk, bringing out an old grey blanket.

"There," he said, throwing it at her, "this should take care of your modesty. Now get changed because that's an order."

She tilted her chin upwards. "And if I don't choose to obey?"

"Then I shall be forced to undress you, myself. You wouldn't want that, would you?"

Kessie longed to hit out at him, he was so unbearably arrogant. Yet she knew he was simply thinking of her own good.

"All right," she said, "turn your back." She

wrapped the coarse blanket round her and slipped her trousers off. She had to admit, she was far more comfortable without them and much warmer.

Brent made the coffee and Kessie took it from him, gratefully warming her fingers around the tin mug.

"Is this hut specifically built for emergencies such as this?" she asked, making an effort at polite conversation. Brent stared at her.

"Bright girl!" His tone was scathing and Kessie sighed, forcing down the angry words that longed to be spoken.

"It's useless, isn't it? I mean you just can't converse with someone who has no manners and none of the social graces, it just isn't possible."

He ignored her and got to his feet, crossing to where the horse was standing docile against the far wall. He took out a pair of trousers from the saddle bag and began to change into his dry clothes with no preliminary explanation.

Kessie lay down on the bunk and closed

her eyes, her face hot. He really was a monster, how could a kindly man like Lars have such a son?

"That's right." His voice came across to her. "Try to get some rest, you look washed out. Anyway, there's nothing else to be done right now, is there?"

She turned her back on him and closed her eyes. She felt suddenly weary, wondering why on earth she had left all that was familiar to her in London to come to this outlandish place in Norway. Tears burned against her lids but she had no intention of letting them fall. She would not give Brent the opportunity to see her at her most vulnerable.

Sleep would not come, however much she tossed and turned, she simply could not get comfortable. Brent seemed fast asleep, curled up on the wooden floor next to the fire. Kessie sat up. The fire seemed to be dying out, perhaps she should do something about it.

Pulling the blanket closer, she slid from the bunk and made her way awkwardly to the pile of wood in the corner. She picked some pieces of twig at random and put them on the fire hoping for a more cheerful blaze. Instead, to her consternation, smoke billowed upwards stinging her eyes and causing her to cough.

"What have you done now?" Brent was up on one elbow, staring at her as though she was all sorts of a fool.

"I just thought I'd keep the fire going, that's all," she said. "I'm cold."

"Can't you even tell the difference between seasoned wood and green wood?" he asked mildly.

Suddenly it was all too much for Kessie and in spite of her reluctance to show her feelings in the presence of this arrogant man, tears began to run down her cheeks and splashed on to her hands.

He paid no attention to her, he simply set about putting the fire to rights, allowing her to sob herself into quietness. She rubbed at her eyes and wrapped the blanket more tightly around herself.

"When the fire has more heat in it I'll

make you a hot drink," he said in a not unkind voice. "Perhaps you should consider returning to England, this isn't civilisation as you see it, you know."

She was too tired to argue with him. She accepted the hot drink when he'd made it and then turned her face to the wall and from sheer exhaustion fell into a deep sleep.

She woke to a sensation of someone shaking her and she looked up to see Brent bending over her, his face copper coloured in the blaze from the fire.

"Are you all right?" he asked. "You seemed to be moaning in pain, is it your ankle?"

She tried to sit up and found that her arms would not support her weight. Her head ached and her teeth were chattering; she felt awful.

"It's nothing to worry about," she said with an effort. "I've had bouts of fever ever since I was a child. I caught something when I went to India with my father once on one of his trips. It will pass in a few hours, it's all right."

She lay back exhausted by the effort of

talking and Brent brushed the tangled hair back from her face, drawing the blanket more closely round her shaking limbs.

"Is there anything I can do to help?" he asked, and there seemed to be concern in his eyes though it may have been nothing more than a reflection from the fire.

"No, nothing, just keep me warm," she whispered. Immediately, he lay down beside her on the bunk, drawing her into his arms. Feebly she tried to protest but he held her fast.

"Look, Kessie," he said, using her name for the first time. "I have no evil intentions, in fact I'm engaged to a very attractive girl, so please rest assured I mean nothing by this, except to help keep us both warm. Now keep still and be sensible."

She relaxed, knowing he was right. Out here in this remote mountain area there were no rules except those of survival.

His hand was warm against the small of her back, holding her so close to him that she could feel his heart beating. She gave in to the warmth and the feeling of languor that was difficult to resist and rested her head against his shoulder. She felt her eyes close and her breath mingled with Brent's so they were like one being and she slept.

She didn't know if she was in the hold of some nightmare or other but it seemed to Kessie that she had a raging thirst. She saw Brent bringing in snow and melting it over the fire, holding the mug to her lips, bathing her face and wrists. His eyes seemed filled with kindness and then when the shivering began again, he held her in his arms once more, pressing her against him as though to give her his strength. And Kessie knew that whatever else might pass between her and this man, she would never forget his care of her this night.

Then it was morning and a pale light filtered in through the small window. Her fever had gone and all she felt was light-headed and weak. She was still locked in Brent's arms and she looked carefully at him. In sleep, his face was serene and softer, his slate-grey eyes hidden by light silky lashes. She knew she should move away from him, dress herself before he woke, save them both embarrassment and yet she was reluctant to break the spell, the illusion of closeness.

Then his eyes were open, looking into hers and Kessie felt the hot colour flood into her cheeks.

"How are you feeling now?" he asked without moving, and his mouth was just above hers, making her heart beat so rapidly, she was sure he must feel it.

"Much better, thanks to you," she said. "I'm really very grateful to you."

"I'll see what the weather's like." Brent moved away from her and suddenly she was cold again.

"Are my clothes dry?" she asked and Brent threw them towards her. He kept his back to her, crouching over the fire, building it up to a cheerful blaze.

"I hope the storm's past," Kessie said, feeling absurd making small talk with the man whose arms she'd lain in all night.

"I'll just put the coffee pot on, then I'll see," Brent said, straightening up. He caught her eye and smiled. "Don't look so nervous, I'm not really such a monster you know."

"Of course not." Kessie looked down at her crumpled suit, it had looked so fresh and fashionable when she'd first put it on. She was aware that her hair was tangled around her face, she must look a pretty picture indeed.

Brent opened the door and all seemed silent. "The storm is over," Brent said with satisfaction. "I'll be able to set off a flare which they will see from the hotel. We'll soon be in the warmth and comfort of civilisation once more."

"But not what you'd call my sort of civilisation?" Kessie couldn't help saying. Brent shook his head.

"I doubt you'll last the pace for a couple of weeks even, there are no city streets to step out on, no colourful shops to amuse you, I hope you realise that."

Kessie felt the warmth and intimacy that had existed between them was gone. She sighed.

"Can't we just set off for the hotel on your horse?" she asked. "I don't really see any point in our waiting here for help to come."

"Ah, but then you don't know the land as I do," Brent said briskly. "The snow is deep and for one horse carrying two people the journey would be doubly hard. No, we wait."

He took something out of the saddle bags. "I'm just going outside to send off a flare," he said. "Perhaps you could see to the coffee?"

They were back on the old hostile footing, now, as though the night had never been, and Kessie nodded.

"Yes, I'll do that," she said curtly and turned away from him as he went outside, closing the door after him.

She forced herself to rise though her legs still trembled with weakness. She held onto the cupboard for a few minutes, trying to steady herself and then she managed to pick up the two cups that held the dregs of last night's coffee.

With difficulty, she made her way to the

door. It might be a good idea, she decided, to scoop snow into the cups and clean them before making fresh drinks.

The door was difficult to open, the casing of ice on the outside making it heavy. Kessie pulled hard and it yielded, letting in a rush of cold air.

Holding her breath, she stepped outside, half closing her eyes against the flurry of snow. With a suddenness that made her scream, she slipped, falling into the banked-up snow at the side of the pathway Brent had made. She bit her lips forcing herself up out of the stinging wetness. Could she do nothing right?

"Had yet another accident?" Brent said, and she saw that the cups she'd dropped were in his hands.

He helped her back into the comparative warmth of the hut and she shook her head, trying to find words that would justify her.

"I don't know how it happened, I suppose I'm just not used to these sort of conditions."

With trembling fingers, Kessie began to

remove her wet clothing. She made an attempt at lightness.

"This is getting to be a habit, my suit will be ruined by the time I've finished with it."

"There are plenty more where that came from," Brent said, his voice suddenly hard. "You could buy a storeful with the money my father paid you for the Danton hotel."

She glanced at him quickly, as she wrapped herself once more in the rough blanket.

"What about it?" she asked. "Was there some reason why you didn't want your father to take on the Danton?"

He gave a short hard laugh. "Oh no, it was nothing to do with me, my father made that perfectly clear, it was entirely his decision and I had to mind my own business."

Kessie was bewildered. "Why are you so angry?" she asked, staring at him as he bent over to pour the coffee into the stained mugs.

"Here!" he handed her one. "Drink it if your stomach isn't too delicate. Though I assure you a few coffee grounds won't hurt you."

"You are not answering my question," Kessie insisted, sitting down on the bunk, trying to push back the waves of dizziness that were sweeping over her.

"I don't have to answer to you," he said. "And really, there is no need to carry the naîve act so far, you don't have to impress me."

"You are impossible!" Kessie said, aware that her voice was shaking. "I just do not understand you."

"There is no necessity for you to do so," Brent said in a flat voice as he put down his coffee. "Now if you will excuse me there are things to be done."

He took the bridle and slipped it on the docile horse, leading the animal outside into the coldness of the air. Kessie watched him through the small window as he exercised the animal, both horse and rider looking magnificent against the whiteness of the snow.

Kessie drank the coffee which was surprisingly good. It seemed to bring some warmth back into her body, giving her strength. She

31

looked carefully among the branches of wood in the corner and picked out some pieces that she judged to be seasoned enough to burn. She wasn't going to make the same mistake again.

Time seemed to pass slowly. She picked up her clothes, which were almost dry, and she began to rub them, fruitlessly trying to erase some of the creases.

Brent returned and nodded with approval when he saw the fire.

"I see you are learning," he remarked and Kessie felt absurdly pleased with the praise, faint though it was.

"I need some cloth," he said, eyeing the jacket in her hand. "I shouldn't think you're likely to wear that again are you?"

She paused for a moment before handing it to him. "No, I suppose not." She wondered what he wanted it for and was amazed when he crumpled it up and began to rub down the heaving flanks of the horse with it.

"Couldn't you have used your own shirt for that?" she asked, feeling somehow that he was laughing at her.

"Why?" he asked, "don't you think the beast wants to be warm and comfortable too?"

She sat down on her bunk again, her knees trembling. Why did he have this strange effect on her? He was a complete stranger to her, and in any case hadn't he told her he was engaged to another girl? The thought suddenly depressed her.

She began to pull on her trousers, suddenly angry with Brent and with herself. The more distance between him and her the better, she decided. Once they were at the hotel she would steer clear of him, of that much she was certain.

The zip jammed and though Kessie tugged at it furiously, it would not move.

"Need any help?" Brent was smiling and she shook her head, determined not to accept his help. She tried to ease the zip back down but it was no good, it was stuck fast. In her efforts, the blanket was dislodged from around her shoulders.

"For heaven's sake!" Brent came over to

her and pushed her hands away from the zip. "If you don't let me help, you'll be there all day!"

He had just finished speaking when the door opened and a gust of cold air made Kessie shiver. To her embarrassment, Lars was blocking the doorway, a strange expression on his face as he saw his son and Kessie apparently in an intimate situation. Behind Lars stood a younger man, a paler version of Brent, and Kessie hazarded a guess that he was a younger brother.

"What's happened?" Lars said, entering the hut. Brent's hands fell away from Kessie's waist and he picked up the blanket, draping it around Kessie's shoulders.

"It would take too long to explain, father," he said, and the younger man stepped forward, his eyes alight with speculation as they rested on Kessie.

"Hello," he said, "I'm Eric." He laughed and glanced towards his father. "I don't really think explanations are necessary, father," he said. "After all you have to be broadminded these days."

"That's enough of that," Lars said in a soft voice, but one which defied argument. "Let's just see about getting Miss Danton safely back to the hotel."

TWO

The hotel Sornefjord was quite small by Kessie's standards but she had to admit that it was the last word in luxury. Apart from that, the mountain-top hotel had a character all its own, set as it was in a mellow old building that had been carefully and tastefully modernised.

Huge log fires dominated the reception rooms while discreet central heating kept the bedrooms at a comfortable temperature.

Kessie was sitting with Lars in his office and even from this viewpoint the panoramic spread of the mountain and the valley far below was breathtaking.

"Ah, we have an enquiry here from a lady film star." Lars was sorting through the mail, hardly looking at Kessie even when he spoke to her. He had been a little stand-offish ever since he had opened the door of the hut and found Kessie and Brent apparently in an intimate embrace. He would listen to nothing she tried to say, and as for Brent he seemed to feel that an explanation was superfluous.

"Lars," she said, making one more attempt, "if you would only let me tell you what happened the day I arrived."

"No." He lifted a big hand, turning his leonine head away from her. "I do not wish to speak of it and as for my son I am disappointed in him."

Kessie sighed. "You make me feel you are disappointed in me, too, Lars, and yet nothing was as it seemed, I was ill and Brent cared for me, there was nothing more."

Her mind took a leap back to the night when she had lain in Brent's arms trembling with fever and yet still aware of the magnetic quality of the man. She had thought of little else and yet she knew that it had meant nothing at all to Brent. He had almost shunned her since they arrived at the hotel. She had seen him with a tall blonde Scandinavian girl several times and guessed she was the fiancée Brent had spoken of.

"Are you listening to me, Kessie?" Lars' voice impinged on her thoughts and she looked at him sharply.

"I'm sorry, Lars," she said quickly. "I wasn't listening, I can't help being upset by your refusal to listen to me."

"Let us concentrate on the business in hand," Lars said almost reproachfully. "The hotel won't run itself, you know."

Kessie felt the rebuke sharply and swallowed hard. "I'm sorry," she repeated. "Please go on with what you were saying."

He handed her a bundle of letters. "Look at these, see if you can sort them out. Most of them are definite bookings. It will be a great deal of work to sort out the room allocations."

"I'm used to that, Lars," Kessie said eagerly, "and I promise I'll do my best to make you proud of me. I managed the Danton single handed when my father was ill, you know that."

"Yes." Lars rose to his feet. "I will leave you to it. Now there are a number of other items that need my attention. See you later, Kessie." He smiled. "Join me for dinner in my rooms, it will be a sort of farewell party. I'll be off on my travels in the morning, I must keep in touch with my other hotels, can't put all my eggs into this one basket, especially as it's balanced so precariously on a mountain top in more ways than one." He moved to the door. "I will see you later."

When she was alone, Kessie stared down at the pile of mail. She didn't mind hard work but the cloud of Lars' disapproval was proving a burden. Still, he seemed to have thawed a little now. After all, she was invited to his farewell dinner.

She forced herself to concentrate on the work before her and began making entries in the booking file in neat, clear handwriting. There was a great deal to be done and when at last she leaned back in her chair and stretched her cramped fingers, she was surprised to see it was growing dark outside.

It didn't take her long to prepare for dinner, however. A quick relaxing shower and ten minutes spent brushing her long hair made her feel almost relaxed. She changed into a long, soft blue dress, and with slightly quickened heart beats made her way along the deeply carpeted corridor towards Lars' suite of rooms.

Brent was standing near the window and at his side was the blonde girl. Kessie smiled at her and was rewarded by an icy look in return. Kessie guessed she must be confronting Brent's fiancée.

"Inga, you haven't been introduced to Kessie Danton yet, have you?"

It was Lars who broke the uncomfortable silence. "Kessie is the daughter of a man who was a good friend to me when I first started out in business. Come along, shake hands with each other!"

In spite of his cheerfulness, Kessie saw that Lars was a little impatient with Inga who still hung back as though reluctant to have anything to do with Kessie.

"I'm very pleased to meet you," Kessie said. "I've been admiring your lovely blonde hair whenever I've seen you from a distance."

"Really?" Inga, in common with Lars and his sons, spoke excellent English with just a trace of what seemed to be an American drawl.

Kessie sat down at the table next to Inga, very conscious of Brent's scrutiny.

"Where is Eric?" Lars said. "I told the boy to be here on time, he knows I hate to be kept waiting."

The door opened and Eric appeared, a broad smile on his face as he caught the gist of his father's words.

"I am on time," he said, seating himself next to Kessie. "Here, look at my watch, Kessie, you'll bear me out that it is only just on the dot of seven thirty, won't you?"

She was at a loss for something to say, very much aware of Eric leaning close to her, his knee touching hers beneath the table. It looked as though she might be going to have trouble with him, he had certainly been giving her speculative looks and winking at her in a horrible, knowing way when he thought no one else was looking.

"Well, let's take your word for it," Lars said. "Tomorrow, as you all know, I'll be going to the city. I want everything to run smoothly here while I am away, now can I depend on you all for that?"

Brent coughed. "Does that mean I won't be going with you, after all, father?"

Lars gave his son a brief look. "I shan't need you, Brent, you can help me more by staying here."

"But father," Brent was leaning forward. "I don't want to be stuck away here for ever, that's not my idea of a job for life."

"Oh, and what do you want then, Brent?" Lars said. "To take over my business from me, is that it?"

Kessie bit her lip, it seemed a family quarrel was developing. She clasped her hands together under the table, and then to her surprise and dismay felt them being covered by Eric's hand.

"You forget, father," Brent said, "some of it is my business, I've put my money into it as you have yours."

"You have put your money into this hotel." Lars turned away from his son, waving his hand. "This should be your concern, you know as well as I do that the other hotels can practically run themselves. I don't need you in any of them, I need you here to make a success of this one."

"To make up for the losses you sustained on the London deal?" Brent said quickly, and Lars became red with anger.

"I will have no more business talk at the table," he said, and Kessie saw Inga put a cautious hand on Brent's arm.

"Yes, father." Brent spoke more quietly. "You're quite right, the dinner table is no place to discuss business."

Kessie was trying to dislodge Eric's imprisoning hand without drawing attention to herself, but without success. She was relieved when the first course was served and he was forced to set her cramped fingers free.

The dinner was not an outstanding success. Kessie felt a complete outsider and as she thought over the angry words that had just passed between Lars and Brent she began to wonder what was the underlying cause for the animosity. Surely it wasn't only the fact that she and Brent had spent the night together in the hut that was angering Lars? No, there must be more to it than that. Brent had mentioned the London deal, and no doubt there was a great deal the men could argue over if they so wished. She was being over-sensitive in feeling that she was the bone of contention.

Inga's attitude didn't soften in the slightest as the evening progressed, in fact it was only Eric who seemed at all keen on even talking to her. Kessie felt very much a stranger and as soon as it was polite to do so, she made an excuse and went to her own room.

She sat down on the bed and closed her eyes, leaning her chin in her hands. Had it all been a great mistake, coming here to Norway? And yet at first the prospects had seemed so bright, a new start in a different country, surrounded, she thought, by a kindly Norwegian family. Well it hadn't turned out at all like that.

Tears fell on to her hands and she brushed them away impatiently. Crying would do no good, she wasn't going to give in without a struggle. She would prove to the entire Tolkelarson family that she could do her job here and do it well. She might then consider returning home and finding something more congenial to do.

She barely slept. Her mind kept turning over the events of the evening from Inga's open hostility to Eric's silly overtures. It hadn't been a happy experience but on the other hand she would be foolish to let such a little thing put her off making a good career for herself.

At last from sheer exhaustion she fell asleep but in the pale morning light she felt heavy eyed and reluctant to get out of bed.

She was just tying on her robe when she heard the soft sounds of horses' hooves outside in the grounds. She went to the window and looked out in time to see Lars and

Brent side by side, riding away from the hotel.

Brent sat high in the saddle, his shoulders broad beneath the cloth of his coat. Something caught in Kessie's throat. Why couldn't she forget what it had been like to lie in his arms? It was no good to feel that she had belonged there. Brent hardly noticed her, and anyway he had the beautiful Inga to keep him happy. She turned away from the window. Well, Brent had obviously persuaded his father to change his mind about going to the city alone. He was obviously going with him and Kessie wondered dismally what the hotel would be like without either of them around. She had the feeling that the coming days would be pretty cheerless.

Eric was in the office before her. He looked up and smiled as she entered and Kessie suddenly felt on her guard. She didn't like the familiar way that Eric's eyes roved over her figure in the neat skirt and jacket she was wearing.

"Good morning," she said briskly. "I see

we have to cope alone, both your father and Brent have left for the city, I take it?"

"Quite correct." Eric smiled at her. "There is no reason to be so formal, can't you and I be friends, Kessie?"

"Of course." Kessie wouldn't look at him; instead she picked up a bundle of letters from the table and glanced through them. Eric took them from her with an apologetic laugh.

"Don't bother, I've already opened the mail and noted down the bookings. There isn't much for you to do here, so why not come with me and have a coffee?"

"All right." Kessie could think of no good reason for refusing. In any case it wouldn't do to be churlish to Eric, not when he was making a good attempt to be on his best behaviour.

The hotel dining room was open for business and as Kessie sat at one of the tables, she couldn't help admiring the decor of the room.

Beyond the rich red carpet, one wall was completely made of glass, giving beautiful views of the mountain peaks.

"It really is a beautiful place." Kessie sighed and Eric glanced at her questioningly.

"Why do you sound so sad? Surely you are pleased to be here in Norway with us?"

Kessie looked at him guardedly. "I hope I'm going to be happy here, Eric," she said. "But that depends on how well I do my job, and if I can persuade your father that there is nothing between Brent and myself."

Eric smiled. "We will talk more when I bring the coffee, wait here and I'll go through to the kitchen and get a tray." He looked round the empty room. "It's all ready and waiting for our guests to arrive. When they do, Kessie, you'll be able to prove to my father how indispensable you are."

She watched him go through the swing doors into the kitchen. He really was being quite sensible and friendly. Perhaps she'd misjudged him and allowed herself to become over-sensitive to his advances. He obviously wished her well, he'd helped her with the bookings already this morning. It was a promising start anyhow.

She smiled at him more warmly as he returned with a tray. He set it down before her and inclined his head.

"You pour, will you? I always get all fingers and thumbs with those little pots and things."

"Look, Eric." Kessie leaned towards him anxiously. "You believe me that there was nothing going on in the hut, don't you?"

She handed him a cup and he took it from her, his eyes looking directly into hers.

"Why do you make so much of it, Kessie?" he asked. "If you'd only let the subject drop perhaps my father would put it all out of his mind too."

His words made good sense and Kessie sat back in her chair with a sigh.

"All right, we'll make a pact not to speak of it again." She drank some of her coffee. "We'd better not stay too long, we've a lot more details to sort out before we can take it easy."

Eric nodded. "Just as you say, Kessie, but

promise me one thing, that you'll let me take you to dinner this evening."

"Take me to dinner, but where?" she said in surprise. "I thought that this hotel was the only one for miles around."

Eric smiled. "Ah, so it is but just ten miles along the ridge, there's a lovely little village, at least it was once a little village, it's now quite a popular ski resort. It would do us both good to get out of the hotel for an hour or two."

"Yes, you could be right," Kessie said. "Just so long as we're not stuck somewhere in a storm!" she added feelingly, and Eric smiled again.

"No, I promise you that we'll get back here safely at quite a reasonable hour. We can be sure that the staff will look after the hotel in our absence. Come along Kessie, say yes."

"It's a date," Kessie said against her better judgement. But she didn't want to antagonise Eric now, not when they seemed to be on a much better footing. "Come on, let's get back to work so that we can go out with an easy conscience."

Later, as she was leaving the office, Kessie saw Inga come into the entrance of the hotel, her long hair tied up in a bright red scarf.

"Hello." Kessie smiled in an attempt to be friendly but Inga did not return the greeting.

"Were you looking for Brent?" Kessie said more coolly. "Because if you are I'm afraid you're going to be disappointed."

"What do you mean?" Inga's eyes flashed as she crossed the carpeted foyer towards Kessie.

"I'm afraid he had to go away on business this morning. I'm sure he means to ring you or something to explain."

"You have no need to make excuses for Brent to me, Miss Danton," Inga said in a voice that was taut with resentment. "I think I know him just a little better than you do."

"I'm sure you do," Kessie responded with a small flicker of anger which she kept under tight control. "I merely thought..."

"Well don't think, not where Brent and I

are concerned," Inga broke in. "Just leave him alone, do you understand me?"

"Brent and I will have to work together," Kessie said after a moment's pause. "Other than that I'm not in the least bit interested in him or you, is that plain?"

She walked away, her hands trembling. This wasn't a very promising start to her stay in Norway, she seemed to be making a new enemy with every day that passed.

She was aware of light footsteps behind her and then Inga's hand was on her shoulder, swinging her round.

"Don't pretend to be a little miss innocent!" she said fiercely. "I know how you spent your first night in Norway, lying in Brent's arms. Oh yes, I know all about that little episode."

"Did Brent tell you himself?" Kessie asked, trying desperately to keep her voice level.

"That's my business!" Inga retorted, and Kessie nodded her head.

"I thought so, you were told the story by someone else and I've a good idea who it was. Well I'd advise you to ask Brent for the correct version of what happened that night. Now are you going to take your hands off my shoulder before I become angry?"

Surprised, Inga moved away and Kessie gave a sigh of relief. She didn't know quite what she'd have done if the girl had refused to release her. She was hardly a match for the tall Norwegian and in any case, she couldn't have started a brawl in the middle of the hotel.

She went to her room. She was furious with Eric because it must have been he who had told Inga about the night in the hut. She should refuse to speak to him until he apologised – yet on the other hand perhaps it would be better to have a quiet little talk with him. Going out with him tonight might prove just the right sort of opportunity.

She dressed carefully in a plain, fine wool skirt and top, tying a green scarf around the neckline to brighten the outfit up a little. She wanted to look smart but not too smart, otherwise Eric might get the idea that she was leading him on. She would have to tread a very fine line with that young man.

He beamed at her when she went downstairs to meet him and he took her arm, tucking it under his.

"We are lucky the weather is clear," he said. "We should have no difficulty driving out to the little village I told you about. It's a beautiful place. But come, you will see for yourself."

The drive was pleasant with the blue of the evening sky high about them and the glimmer of moonlight on water below in the valley.

"It really is a beautiful country," Kessie said warmly. "I wish..." Her words trailed away and Eric glanced at her in open curiosity.

"What is it you wish, Kessie? Come alone, you can surely tell me."

"It's just that I seem to have started so badly," Kessie said, feeling a little dispirited. "I know that your father thinks badly of me and I'm sure he is angry with Brent too, and all for no good reason!"

"Oh, forget about all that," Eric said. "Look, you can see the lights of the village twinkling and see how fine the mountain peaks look in the moonlight!"

The inn was small and picturesque with huge log fires and dark beams overhead. Kessie looked around her in appreciation, feeling a little more cheerful.

"It's lovely," she said. "Shall we sit over near the fire? It looks so warm and inviting."

Eric took her coat and hung it on a peg, smiling down at her in such a friendly way that she began to wonder if she'd been misjudging him.

"We shall go into dinner in just a few minutes," Eric said, sitting opposite her, leaning across the table, his hand almost touching hers. "I must say you look very lovely, the typical cool English lady."

She stared at him wondering if there was any sarcasm behind his words, but his eyes were clear.

"Eric," she said slowly. "Did you tell Inga about the first night I arrived here?"

"I don't know what you mean," Eric said

briskly. "I have not mentioned it to anyone, why should I?"

She tried to tell from his face if he was speaking the truth.

"Well, Inga was at the hotel today and she is obviously very angry about it. I suppose I can't really blame her, not if she doesn't know the facts."

"Possibly my father thought it correct to tell her," Eric said a little reluctantly. "He believes in straight speaking."

That possibility had not occurred to Kessie. She thought about it and it did seem quite likely that Lars would speak of it to the girl, if he thought it was for her own good.

"Your father and Brent don't get on very well, do they?" Kessie said thoughtfully, and Eric shook his head with a rueful smile.

"No, they don't! I think they are too much alike. Brent has a quick temper, just like my father, and they both want to be the boss." He shrugged. "As for me, I'm content to let them fight it out between them."

Kessie had the uncomfortable feeling that

she was listening to tales out of school, and neatly she changed the subject.

"Does Inga live at the hotel?" she asked and Eric shook his head.

"No, my father does not think that a very good idea but she does come to stay at whatever hotel we may be working at, just for a few days."

"Do you mean that you travel around from hotel to hotel most of the time?" Kessie asked, and Eric smiled.

"Of course, though usually we split it up and pay unexpected visits so that the staff are kept constantly on their toes; or so my father thinks."

It was a relief to Kessie to realise that Eric wouldn't be constantly at her side, but then neither would Brent and that thought was a little more disturbing.

The dinner was very pleasant, the food well cooked and beautifully presented.

"It really is lovely here," Kessie said, glancing around her, and Eric touched her hand briefly.

"Yes, lovely," he murmured, but he was

looking directly at her.

"Was your father's idea to provide alternative accommodation for people who wanted to come up here to ski?" Kessie asked, trying to keep the conversation businesslike.

"I suppose so," Eric shrugged. "But I don't really want to talk about that now. Come along, Kessie, relax can't you!"

She smiled and glanced at her watch. "Well just for a minute, and then we'd better be starting back for the hotel. It's quite a long drive you know."

"All right, we'll start back in just a moment," Eric said. "Don't worry, Kessie, I won't eat you!"

"I'm sorry to be a wet blanket, Eric," Kessie said, "but you see I'm a little tired, I didn't sleep too well last night and I think it's catching up on me now."

To her relief, he rose and gave her a mock bow. "My dear, we will leave this instant."

It was crisp and clear and the sky overhead was ablaze with stars. Kessie shrugged herself into her coat and waited for Eric to open the car door for her.

He glanced at her and smiled and as she slipped into her seat, Kessie sighed. It would be good to get back to the hotel and have a relaxing shower before going to bed.

Eric started the car and put it into gear and it moved slowly forward before giving a jerk and gliding to a stop.

"What's wrong?" Kessie asked dryly. "Not out of petrol, are we?"

"No," Eric shook his head in bewilderment. "It's not that, but whatever it is, the darn thing won't start again."

Kessie's concern grew as Eric slid out of the car and opened up the bonnet. After a few moments, he returned and shook his head.

"It's no good," he said. "We'll have to have someone to look at it in the morning."

"What?" Kessie said. "We can't stay here until morning, it's impossible."

"There's nothing impossible about it, Kessie," Eric said, "and at least you'll have a comfortable inn this time, not a ramshackle mountain hut."

Kessie really wanted to cry. She had the strongest feeling that Eric had done this on purpose. What on earth would Brent think of her after this?

THREE

As soon as she was back inside the inn, Kessie telephoned the hotel. She could hear the ringing go on and on and despaired of any of the staff hearing when at last the line clicked.

"Hello?" It was Inga's voice and Kessie's spirits dropped, she'd hoped that one of the reception clerks would have answered. It was not going to be easy to explain the situation to the hostile Norwegian girl.

"Kessie Danton here," she said briskly. "We've had a little trouble with the car, it seems it can't be repaired until morning so could you ask one of the night staff to make sure the hotel is safely locked up."

There was silence for a moment and then

Inga's voice, full of amused incredulity, came back over the line.

"You are not trying the same trick with the younger brother, are you?" she said bluntly, and Kessie bit her lip in anger.

"It is no trick," she said in clipped tones. "Just an unfortunate accident. Please don't try to make something out of it."

"I'll leave that sort of thing to you," Inga laughed. "Brent will probably be ringing me any time now, I'll explain the situation to him, he's bound to understand."

Kessie closed her eyes. This was the last thing she wanted. She didn't know why, but she wanted Brent to think well of her. Suddenly she felt very tired.

"Oh, do your worst!" she said, and put the receiver back with a bang.

She knew it was foolish of her to antagonise Inga even more than she already had, but it was difficult to keep her temper in the circumstances.

"I've booked us in," Eric said, coming towards her smiling, and suddenly she wanted to hit out at him. She closed her eyes for a moment, trying to count to ten.

"Thank you. If you'll give me the key, I'll go to my room," she said as coldly as she could.

"Oh, this isn't that sort of an inn," Eric said. "It's more what you in your country would call a motel. We have each a little chalet to go to. Come, I will see you safely to yours."

Instinctively, Kessie knew she was going to have trouble with Eric.

"No that's all right," she said quickly. "I'm sure I can find my own way."

"Nonsense!" Eric took her arm and led her out into the crisp air. Kessie shivered, wishing she was anywhere but here at this particular moment.

"Here we are," Eric said, putting the key in the lock and pushing the door open. "After you."

"No, Eric," Kessie said firmly. "I'm not inviting you in, it's far too late and I suddenly feel dreadfully tired."

Eric's face tightened. "Don't be silly, Kessie, surely it won't do any harm if I come inside for just a few minutes?"

"It won't look very good for either of us," she said evenly. "No, it's best if you leave now."

"Why are you treating me like this, Kessie?" Eric said, putting his hand on her arm. "I just want to be friendly, surely you can trust me?"

"Of course I can." Kessie managed to smile. "But you know how people can put the wrong interpretation on such a situation as this. Good night."

She closed the door and leaned against it, her heart beating swiftly. She listened intently for a moment and was relieved to hear Eric's footsteps crunching away on the gravel driveway. She sat on the bed, her hands shaking. That was a close call, she would have to be careful in future not to allow such a situation to arise.

It was difficult to sleep. She kept imagining the way Inga would tell Brent about the events of the night. She would be only too delighted to let him think the worst.

She stared into the darkness, picturing

Brent's lean face. She remembered then how she'd felt lying close in his arms. It was as though she belonged there.

Impatiently, she thumped her pillow. That line of thought would get her exactly nowhere.

In the morning, Eric seemed to have recovered his good spirits and Kessie smiled in relief. She'd half expected him to be morose and reproachful.

"It's going to be a lovely day," he said. "It seems spring is really here at last."

"We'd better get back to the hotel as soon as possible," Kessie said. "We'll be opening for business in a few days time and there's still a great deal to do."

"I know," Eric shrugged, "but can't you think of anything else but business, Kessie?" He touched her hair lightly. "You're much too beautiful to be a career girl."

"Thanks for the compliment," she said lightly. "Come on, let's get started right away."

"Get started," Eric laughed. "That's a rare bit of optimism if you ask me. Perhaps the car isn't ready yet."

Kessie looked at him suspiciously. "You have had someone to look at it, haven't you?" she asked quickly, and Eric smiled.

"Relax, it's being seen to right now. We won't be here long, I promise, but long enough to go for a walk perhaps?"

"I'm sorry, Eric," Kessie said, "but I think we should stay right here, and make sure the job on the car is being done."

"Don't be silly!" Eric laughed. "I'm not going to eat you, it's broad daylight. Come along, this weather is too lovely to waste."

"Oh, all right," Kessie said, "but just a short walk. I'm anxious to get back to the hotel as soon as possible. It's our responsibility after all to see that everything runs smoothly while your father is away."

Reluctantly, she began to walk beside Eric across the narrow mountain road. The sun was warm on her shoulders though some of the higher peaks of the mountain were still iced with snow.

In any other circumstances she might have enjoyed a chance to see some of the exquisite scenery but right now she was too much on edge.

"You're a strange girl, Kessie," Eric remarked, and she glanced at him, keeping her expression one of polite interest.

"Oh, in what way?" She suddenly thought how pompous she sounded but she was still annoyed with Eric for landing her in such an invidious position.

"Difficult to get close to," Eric said. "You have the typical English reserve. Yet you weren't so reserved with my brother."

Kessie was suddenly past caution. "How dare you keep inferring things about me!" she said hotly. "Nothing happened that night, why won't you accept that?"

She turned and began walking back the way they'd come and after a moment, Eric caught up with her.

"All right, Kessie," Eric said. "I apologise. There now, will you say I'm forgiven?"

"Please don't bring it up again, ever," Kessie said, trying to calm herself.

As they approached the inn, Eric suddenly put his arm around her shoulder.

"I was wrong," he said contritely. "I'm really sorry, Kessie. Will you tell me that my apology is accepted?"

"Yes, I suppose so," she said ungraciously, and then suddenly as she looked up, her heart missed a beat as she saw Brent standing in the sunshine outside the inn watching them approach.

"I came to fetch you," he said briskly. "I wasn't sure if the car would be fixed today so I was taking no chances."

There was sarcasm in his voice and his eyes as they looked into Kessie's were hostile.

"But I thought you were in the city with Lars!" Kessie said. "How did you get back so quickly?"

"I travelled through the night," Brent said. "Father insisted on it." His glance reached Eric. "He wants you to take my place in the city and I suggest you get there as quickly as you can. He's in no mood to be kept waiting."

"He's angry?" Kessie asked, her heart in her throat. Brent gave a small, mirthless laugh.

"I think you could safely say that." He moved away from them and gave instructions over his shoulder in a curt voice.

"I'll take Kessie in the Land Rover with me and you, Eric, had better only stop long enough at the hotel to pick up a few things. Father wants immediate action."

Kessie sat uncomfortably cramped in the seat beside Brent. Somehow she couldn't relax and lean back in her seat.

"Well?" she said at last as the ribbon of road wound away under the wheels of the Land Rover.

"Well what?" Brent glanced at her, his expression not softening in the slightest.

"You apparently have already judged me and found me wanting," she said, trying to keep her feelings of despair out of her voice. "Why don't you even try asking me what happened?"

"I asked the mechanic," Brent said. "He told me there was nothing at all wrong with the car, that the worst damage the car had suffered was a flooded engine. That is not enough to stop anyone from driving it ten miles."

"I suppose you will believe that I knew this," Kessie said, searching her mind for the right thing to say. "But it's not true, I know nothing about car engines and I accepted Eric's word that there was something wrong."

Brent's silence was like an insult and Kessie stared up at him, jutting her chin forward, emphasising her words.

"You above all people know how deceptive appearances can be. Can't you take my word for it that I had no wish to stay the night at the inn, I just wanted to get back to the hotel and do my job?"

"If Lars doesn't cool down you may not have a job for very much longer."

Kessie could have hit him. "I suppose you felt it your duty to tell him about Eric and me being out all night?" she said cuttingly and he raised his eyebrows.

"As it happens I didn't have to tell him. Inga telephoned me and it was Lars who answered the call."

It was a small thing but it made Kessie feel a little better. She hadn't liked to think of Brent telling tales out of school. It wasn't in character at all.

In miserable silence, she endured the rest of the drive back to the Sornefjord. It was a relief to be able to hurry away to the privacy of her own room. Once there, she lay on the bed and gave way to the pent-up tears that had ached to be shed as she'd sat at Brent's side in the Land Rover. It just wasn't fair! None of this was her fault and yet she seemed to be coming out looking like a scarlet woman!

She sat up after a while and dried her tears. She would just have to see Lars when he returned and make him listen to her. She wouldn't let any of this get her down, she would do her job and do it well, show everyone that she was capable of being a good manager.

The opening day of the Sornefjord came round almost too quickly, but to Kessie's relief the first of the guests booked in with no trouble except for a few grumbles about the long journey up the mountain.

Kessie wondered if there was a way around this. She was determined to put her mind to the problem, there just had to be a solution somewhere.

Brent made himself inconspicuous but Kessie was aware of his presence all the time as he moved around in the background, watching her, making sure that all went smoothly. At least she'd have the satisfaction of having done her job well, she told herself. Not even Brent could fault her on this.

He came up to her when the first flurry of bookings was over.

"Have you some free time now?" he asked and she looked at him in surprise.

"Yes, do you want to talk to me?" She looked away quickly from his compelling grey eyes, telling herself she was a fool to care what he thought of her.

"We could perhaps have lunch," he suggested in his rather stilted English. "It would make for a much more relaxed atmosphere between us perhaps."

"Aren't you lunching with Inga?" As

usual, she added silently to herself. Inga had avoided Kessie like the plague and this was a state of affairs that had suited Kessie very well.

"No, she has gone to see my father. She will be away for a little while," Brent said by way of a brief explanation.

"And I'll do for a little light relief in her absence?" Kessie said, aware that she sounded cutting, but unable to stop herself from making the obvious remark.

"I merely wished to talk about the hotel," Brent said coldly, "but if it doesn't suit you then forget it."

"No, I'm sorry," Kessie said impulsively. "It was childish of me to burst out like that. I'd very much like to have lunch with you."

Brent smiled and Kessie's heart skipped a beat. She knew she was trembling as she preceded Brent into the dining room.

No sooner had they begun to eat, however, than Kessie was approached by one of the waiters.

"You're needed in reception, Miss Danton." The man gave her an apologetic smile and Kessie rose to her feet at once.

"Excuse me," she said to Brent, hoping he would remain where he was. Instinct was telling her that something had gone wrong.

The commotion in reception confirmed Kessie's worst fears and she stared at the tall elegant woman who seemed to be holding court, surrounded by luggage and hot-faced hotel staff.

"There seems to be a double booking," the desk clerk whispered anxiously to Kessie and held out the register for her to see.

"Please come and sit down in the lounge," Kessie said smoothly, approaching the woman with a smile. "I'm sure you'd like a cup of coffee while you're waiting."

Large eyes flashed towards Kessie, followed by a smile of utmost charm.

"I'm Andrea Davidson, you may have heard of me? This is a charming place, or it will be when I'm given the keys to my suite."

This must be the film star Lars had mentioned, Kessie decided, and her mind went through the list of bookings she herself had made. Andrea Davidson certainly wasn't one of them, Eric must have been responsible.

Kessie led her through to the lounge and as a tray of coffee was promptly put before them, poured a cup first for Andrea Davidson and then one for herself. She wondered briefly what Brent would be making of her long absence but then the film star was speaking.

"I don't know how I managed that dreadful ride up the mountain." She swung back her long hair. "If I hadn't learnt to ride for one of my film parts I don't know how I'd have coped with the journey."

"It's so picturesque, however," Kessie said, automatically defending the hotel. "And of course it does tend to limit the quota of guests so that the place is kept fairly exclusive."

Even as she spoke, Kessie was going over in her mind the order of the bookings she'd made. Where could she have gone wrong?

"I do like a hotel to be fussy about the sort of people they take," Andrea was saying.

"In my profession, you can't be too careful about the company you keep, the newspapers are always ready to pounce on anything that doesn't look perfectly ordinary."

"It must be difficult." Kessie glanced over her shoulder, wondering if she could escape and run through the guest list again and try to find the error that somehow she must have made. It angered her to think that she'd been so careless; it simply wasn't in character at all and how would a double booking look to her employer? It was the sort of mistake that no manageress should ever make.

"Have you ever thought of going into films, dear?" Andrea said. "There are distinct possibilities about you. What did you say your name was?"

"Kessie, if you want to be informal. Kessie Danton." She sat on the edge of her chair, trying desperately to think of some reason for getting away but before should could make a move, Andrea was speaking again.

"You're not listening to me, I'm trying to give you good advice here." She tapped

Kessie's arm. "Your hair now, it really is quite pretty, so why don't you curl it around your face? It would improve your appearance such a lot."

"Well thank you," Kessie said with a trace of irony that was quite lost on Andrea. "But it has to be pinned up, at least while I'm working."

Andrea nodded sympathetically. "I suppose you're right, but when you have some free time, try out my suggestion. I'm sure you'd be delighted with the results."

Kessie got up swiftly, taking advantage of the momentary pause in the conversation.

"Do excuse me for just a minute," she said. "I think I'll order another pot of coffee."

Andrea opened her mouth as though to speak but Kessie pretended not to notice and walked quickly away.

"What on earth's happened?" she said to the desk clerk, "I just do not understand a double booking happening so early in the season."

The clerk shrugged, "I know but there is

nothing I can do about it, Miss Danton."
The man looked at her carefully. "You
realise we usually keep a room vacant in our
other hotels for just this sort of contingency."

"And we have not kept such a room?"
Kessie said through set lips. "Well leave it
with me, I'll sort everything out."

She spoke with far more confidence than
she felt. She knew it hadn't been her error,
it had been Eric's, and yet the ultimate
responsibility lay with her. She sighed, this
was just another reason for Lars to regret
taking her on here.

She went to the office and looked through
the files. There was no doubt about it, they
were double booked and there was no other
suite of rooms of the same standard to offer
the film star. Except her own rooms, of
course. Kessie felt almost light-headed with
relief. She would give up her rooms, that
was the only thing she could do. Where she
would stay herself, she had no idea.

Quickly, she rang through to the house-
keeper. "This is Miss Danton here," she

said. "Would you please clear my belongings out of my suite and have someone change the linen and generally clean the place up. Oh, and perhaps a few flowers might be possible?"

She sighed as she replaced the receiver. Well, that took care of Andrea Davidson, but where she herself would sleep she didn't dare think.

She returned to the lounge and Andrea by now had quite a crowd of admirers surrounding her. When she saw Kessie she waved her hand.

"Oh, my dear, I wondered where you'd got to but as you see, I've had no time to be bored."

Self-consciously, Kessie walked through the fringe of admirers and seated herself beside Andrea.

"Your room will be ready in just a few minutes," she said quietly. "We have just been putting some extra finishing touches to it."

At that moment, Brent came into the room and made his way towards them.

Kessie was acutely aware of his tall lean body as he stopped beside her.

"There seems to be some delay with your room, I understand," he spoke directly to Andrea. "I can't apologise enough for any inconvenience you have been caused."

Andrea took in his tanned face and blonde hair in one quick glance and responded to Brent's smile that was obviously intended to charm, and succeeded admirably.

"Well, I am being looked after beautifully," she said, and rose from her seat taking Brent's arm in a proprietary way that set Kessie's teeth on edge. "Perhaps you would like to show me personally to my room?" She took the key from Kessie.

"My pleasure," Brent said, leaning towards her and smiling. "After all you have been kept waiting quite some time, a regrettable oversight on the part of the management."

His glance flickered over Kessie and she knew that his criticism was directed at her. Her cheeks flamed, it wasn't fair! Brent was prejudging her, as usual.

Turning, she hurried away from the curious glances of the guests who were waiting to have their room numbers, and inwardly sent up a prayer that there would be no more double bookings. She hurried towards the office. She really would have to have this out with Eric. He would have to be far more careful in future.

The office was empty. Frustrated, Kessie banged her hand on the desk. The door behind her swung open and Brent stood there, his eyes regarding her steadily.

"Well, that was a fiasco, wasn't it?" he said. "Double booked on our first week of opening. I wonder how many other hotels would find themselves in such an awkward situation."

Kessie tried desperately to think of something to say. It wasn't on to put the blame on Eric even though the error had been his.

"Well, the problem is solved, so please let the matter drop, will you?" she said at last.

"Fine, but where are you going to sleep, on one of the sofas in the lounge?"

"Leave that to me!" she snapped. "That's

my worry not yours."

He shrugged and left the room, and she stared at the closed door intently as if it could give her the answer to her problem.

FOUR

Kessie sat in Brent's small room at the top of the hotel and stared around her, taking in the utter lack of frills both in the decor and the personal possessions that surrounded her.

It was Brent who had solved the problem of where she was going to sleep, leaving his decision until the very last moment as though to keep her in suspense.

"I'll move into Eric's room," he said briskly. "He shouldn't be back for a few days at least, and even if he does return unexpectedly there are two single beds, we'd manage."

It had been humbling to have to accept his offer but there had been no alternative. Now as she moved towards the window and stared at the grounds of the hotel far below, she felt that she'd failed miserably. Brent must think her unfit to manage a hotel at all.

Below the plateau, the valley fell away in soft folds of misty blue and grey, and lovely though it was, Kessie couldn't help the sudden surge of homesickness that brought a suspicion of tears to her eyes.

She had no difficulty in handling the management of the Danton but then the hotel in London was an established one, running on oiled wheels with experienced staff to back her.

She was startled by a sudden knocking on the door and then Brent was in the room, filling it, towering over Kessie as he moved towards her.

"I'm sorry to disturb you," he said, "I forgot to collect my shaving things, I won't take a minute."

"Help yourself," Kessie said, sitting down in a chair, her legs suddenly too weak to support her.

He looked down at her and smiled. "Don't

take what happened too much to heart," he said in a surprisingly kind voice. "A double booking isn't the end of the world after all. Perhaps I was a little hasty, acting as though it was some crime. I'm sorry."

His words disarmed her and Kessie stared up at Brent almost as though she didn't know him. She searched her mind for something to say but the words wouldn't come.

"I hope you haven't been upset by the incident." Brent studied her face, his hands reaching out, catching her chin so that she was forced to look into his eyes.

"You've been crying." He pulled her suddenly to her feet and drew her close to him. "Silly girl, there's no need of tears, it's not that bad."

"Your father will think it is." She forced the words out though her voice was shaking.

"Don't worry about it," Brent insisted, drawing her closer to him. "You've got to be tough if you're going to be a business woman, you know."

She tried to pull free of him but he held

her tightly. She wished he wouldn't be kind, not now at this moment, she just couldn't take it.

He leaned towards her and his lips brushed hers. Sharply, she drew away but he held her fast, his mouth covering hers again, this time with more passion.

She stood quite still, as though mesmerised, as he kissed her deeply. Suddenly, she jerked herself free.

"What do you think you're doing?" she said, her face hot. "Haven't you forgotten about Inga?"

She hated the way she allowed him to stir her emotions. He was merely amusing himself, passing a little time.

"I'd better go." He moved to the door and stood for a moment, looking at her. Kessie pressed her hands together to stop them from shaking, wishing passionately that he would come back and take her in his arms again.

The door closed behind him and she flung herself on the bed, struggling with mixed emotions. She must be out of her mind.

Brent was a stranger, how could she feel this way about him?

She sat up and put her hands to her cheeks. "I love him!" she whispered incredulously. She couldn't escape the knowledge that Brent was the only man ever to arouse such deep and wonderful emotions within her, but she would make quite sure that he never found out about her feelings.

She hardly saw Brent at all the next day, which was something of a relief. She wasn't convinced that she had her feelings under control. After the problems of the previous day, the hotel seemed to be smoothly running itself, and Kessie was free to go over the booking forms, putting them into order, and she was hardly surprised to find that the error had been Eric's.

There was a knock on the office door and then it was opened by Andrea, who smiled brightly, her hair swinging on her shoulders as she peered into the room.

"Ah, there you are, working away like a little beaver. Don't you ever have any fun?" She didn't wait for an invitation but sat herself in a chair, crossing one slim leg over the other.

"Can I help you?" Kessie asked, a little nonplussed by the woman's attitude.

"I hope so, darling," Andrea said extravagantly. "I want to know if you can put on a party for me at the hotel."

Kessie was thoughtful for a moment. "Yes, I don't see any difficulty there. When would you like it?"

"As soon as possible," Andrea smiled. "And I want it held round the swimming pool, it's such a marvellous, wonderful place, like something out of a fairy tale. Those palm trees at the water's edge and the lovely hot temperature, just what I like."

It was an unusual request but not one impossible to fulfil, Kessie thought.

"I think that can be arranged," Kessie smiled. "Perhaps you could give me an idea of the sort of menu you'd like, and I'd need some idea of the number of people you wish to invite."

"Oh, but everyone in the hotel, my dear Kessie," Andrea smiled, "and that includes the staff, of course."

Kessie blinked. "That's over-generous, isn't it?" She saw Andrea smile mischievously.

"That's the way I give parties, my dear, and I won't be paying out a brass farthing!"

Kessie shrugged. "Well, that's your business of course." She opened a drawer. "Here are some specimen menus. If you could choose which one you'd prefer, it would at least be a starting point."

Andrea quickly flipped through the sheaf of papers. "Oh, I think I'll leave all that to you," she said after a few minutes. "I'm sure your choice will be excellent." She rose to her feet. "See you later, perhaps we could have coffee together or something."

She left the room as suddenly as she'd entered it and Kessie breathed a deep sigh. Andrea Davidson was certainly going to add colour to the life of the hotel. It was only to be hoped that it was not the wrong kind.

The days passed by quickly and Kessie found that if she avoided Brent, she could cope quite well with the business of running the hotel. He seemed as eager as she was to keep a distance between them but she was forced to approach him at last to consult him about the proposed party.

He was nowhere to be found in the main rooms of the hotel and Kessie guessed that she would have to go to his room. With swiftly beating heart, she knocked on his door and stepped back a pace as it was opened at once.

"Oh, I'm sorry to trouble you but if you could spare me a moment." She followed him into the room and saw that it was slightly larger than the one he'd vacated to her but similar in shape and design.

"Excellent view from the window," Brent remarked, and Kessie coloured, aware that he'd noticed her interest in the room.

"I'm sorry," she said, "I won't keep you long, it's about this party that Andrea intends giving. Do you think I should have the heating lowered a little? It will be exceptionally warm around the pool with a large crowd in the place."

Brent smiled. "But I believe everyone will

be in swimming costumes, will they not?" He shook his head. "Not my idea of a comfortable way to dine but at least it's different."

Kessie stared at Brent in dismay. "Good heavens! I didn't realise!" She stared at him doubtfully. "Perhaps I should try to put her off that idea. It may not be one that would appeal to your father."

"You are in charge, Kessie," Brent shrugged, "and Miss Davidson believes you have approved her idea. It would be difficult to change things at this stage."

"Oh, dear." Kessie stared at Brent in dismay. "It looks as though I've made yet another blunder." She moved to the door and Brent opened it for her in silence. She glanced up at him, trying to read something in his slate grey eyes, but it was impossible.

"Well," she said, pausing, "I suppose the party will have to go ahead then, and I'd better leave the temperature of the pool as normal."

"If that's your decision," Brent said, a little smile on his face.

"You're enjoying this, aren't you?" Kessie said, suddenly angry, "and you're determined not to help me one iota!"

He smiled broadly then. "I'm looking forward to seeing you in a swim suit, Kessie, though I can't say it will be the first time I've seen you with very little on."

"You're impossible!" Kessie stormed away from him and along the corridor to her own room. It was all right for Brent to laugh about it all but she would be the one to carry the can if anything went wrong.

As it turned out, she was late arriving at the pool on the evening of the party and everything seemed to be in full swing. Kessie stood in the background, aware that everything looked beautiful, and the knowledge gave her a sense of satisfaction.

Small tables and chairs had been placed along the poolside, giving the effect of an open air café. Lights shimmered on the water and soft music played discreetly in the background.

Excited screams came from the pool itself as several of the guests dived into the clear water. Then Kessie caught sight of Andrea. She was on a chaise longue, her hair hanging over her bare brown shoulders, a tiny scrap of red bikini barely covering her supple figure.

No wonder she'd chosen such a setting for her party, it was one in which she could be sure of looking her best.

"Kessie!" Andrea's voice rose in excitement. "Come here at once, I've a bone to pick with you."

Reluctantly, Kessie went over to where Andrea was lying, and dropped into a sitting position beside her.

"Yes, what is it? I hope you haven't any complaints about the food or the service," Kessie said lightly.

"No, of course not!" Andrea smiled brilliantly. "Everything is beautiful, but it's you, my dear, you haven't entered into the spirit of the thing at all. Why aren't you wearing a swim suit?"

"I hardly think it would be appropriate in the circumstances," Kessie said. "I'm not really a guest, just the manager of the hotel."

"Oh come along now." Andrea sat up and pushed back her long hair. "I know you're off duty, so go and put on a bikini. Here, I've a spare one, be a sport, you look really overdressed among all the other people. Let your hair down for once!"

"She's right, you know." Brent stood beside them, tall and muscular in his swimming trunks. He grinned. "You do look out of place here. In fact you stick out like a sore thumb. For heaven's sake join in the fun. After all no one is going to need you, the guests are all here."

Kessie didn't like to say that she hated the water and was absolutely terrified of it. She got to her feet, reluctantly taking the swimming suit from Andrea.

In the changing room, Kessie stared at her reflection in dismay. The bikini was unbelievably small by any standards and she felt she couldn't possibly appear in public wearing it. She looked around her, wondering if she should dress and slip away before anyone noticed she was gone.

"Hey!" Andrea looked round the door, a

smile on her face as she saw that Kessie was changed.

"You're ready, good, we've all been waiting for you." She caught Kessie's arm and drew her back into the crowded area of the pool.

Brent's eyes were inscrutable as they rested on Kessie and she felt her cheeks burn in embarrassment. She went to the side of the pool and sat down, staring into the water, wondering if she had the courage to slip into it as a means of concealing herself. She could always make the excuse that she was cold and uncomfortable in her wet suit and go and put her clothes on again.

"So, you decided to join in the spirit of the occasion." Brent sat down beside her, his warm arm touching hers, and Kessie felt herself shiver at the contact.

"It seems I had no option," she managed to say. "Andrea can be very persuasive when she puts her mind to it."

"I've noticed," Brent said dryly, "but at least try to smile, make a pretence of enjoying yourself even if you're bored stiff with the company you're in."

"Oh, but I'm not bored!" Kessie said quickly. "It's just that I don't like the water very much, in fact it scares me out of my mind. I was just trying to pluck up the courage to go in when you came along."

"You don't have to participate to that extent if you don't want to," Brent said cheerfully, "but if you'd like to learn to swim, I'd be happy to teach you."

"That's kind of you." Kessie looked at him uncertainly. "But I'm sure to make a fool of myself."

"Don't be silly." Brent got to his feet and held out his hand to her. "Come along, we'll go in at the shallow end. Take everything easy, step by step, you'll see there's nothing to be afraid of."

It was a good feeling to have Brent's strong fingers holding hers and Kessie knew she could trust him not to do anything foolish like pushing her under the water. She went with him and gasped as her feet touched the water's edge.

"It's colder than I thought," she said,

feeling a moment of panic as the water lapped at her legs. She took a deep breath and followed Brent trustingly until the water was touching her waist.

"It's not so bad, is it?" Brent smiled his encouragement, and in response, Kessie managed a smile though she was terrified that at any moment, she might slip and be swallowed up by the cold blueness.

Brent put his arm around her waist. "Now do you think you could lean forward?" he said. "Try to sort of lie out on the surface. I'll hold you, it's all right."

His touch was sending shivers through Kessie that had nothing to do with the cold. She took a deep breath and lifted her feet from the bottom, relying solely on Brent to hold her afloat.

Water lapped into her mouth and she jerked away spluttering. Immediately, Brent had both arms around her, setting her on her feet, once more.

"There's no need to panic," he said calmly. "It won't harm you if you swallow a little water. Just take it slowly and we'll try again."

Kessie's confidence was growing. She smiled up at Brent and it was as though he could sense her feelings.

"It's good, isn't it?" he said. "The feeling of just being almost weightless, letting the water take you over. It's an excellent way to relax." He looked at her quizzically. "And I certainly think you need to relax occasionally, don't you?"

Before Kessie could think of an answer, she heard her name being called and she looked up to see Andrea waving to her from the side of the pool.

"Come along," she was saying. "It's about time I had swimming lessons now!"

Kessie moved away from the circle of Brent's arms but the water buffeted her and she was washed against him. He held her close for a moment and then she realised that she was clinging to him.

"You'd better help me out," she said with a rueful laugh, "I'm like a stranded porpoise without your help."

He drew her towards the steps and helped her out of the water and Kessie smiled at him gratefully.

"Thanks," she said, "I think I might be less timid next time I try to swim."

Andrea sauntered towards them, her figure stunning in the silk of her bikini, her hair flowing down her back.

"I don't see why you should have all the fun!" Andrea said pouting. "I want Brent to teach me to swim, too. Come along, Brent, I'm not letting you escape."

Andrea slipped her arm in his and Kessie turned away, unable to bear the searing pain of jealousy that surged through her.

Andrea was making such a fuss that by now everyone's attention was riveted on her as she clung to Brent's broad shoulders, screaming a little as he drew her along in the water.

Kessie glanced back and it was quite obvious that Andrea could swim perfectly well. She twisted away from Brent, splashing water over him and with a graceful movement, glided through the water like a slim brown fish.

Kessie picked up Andrea's towel and dried

her face, hiding in the soft folds, trying to compose herself. She still tingled from Brent's touch and she had been amazed how close she'd felt to him in those few moments of intimacy in the water. Why did Andrea have to spoil it? She could have her pick of the men in the party or anywhere else for that matter. Kessie pushed back her hair and ran her fingers through it, flicking droplets of water around her.

"Hey!" a voice at her side said, and she looked up into a craggy, humorous face.

"I'm sorry," Kessie said quickly, "did I drench you?" She tried to place the man. He must be one of the guests and yet she was sure she'd never seen him before.

"I'm just a little damp around the edges," he said, holding out a hand to her. "Jonathon Finch, I'm from London."

"Oh, so am I originally," Kessie said, smiling warmly. "I'm Miss Danton, Kessie Danton, I manage this hotel."

"I see, that's interesting. You don't somehow expect to see a woman in that position," his eyes looked her over, "especially one as attractive as you, if I might say so."

Kessie felt her colour rise. "Oh, I'm not usually as informal as this," she laughed. "It's just a sort of special occasion."

"I know," he smiled. "I should do, I'm Andrea's publicity man."

"Oh?" Kessie looked up at him in surprise. "I'm going to turn the tables on you now," she said with a smile. "I didn't expect to see a man in such a position."

"Oh, our Andrea wouldn't have a woman working for her, they wouldn't get on for more than five minutes at a stretch!" He laughed. "But she has a definite way with the men as you can see for yourself."

Kessie looked to where Andrea was standing, almost up to her neck in water, her arms holding Brent's fair head close to her own dark one.

"She seems to be enjoying herself," Kessie said with difficulty, and Jonathon Finch nodded.

"Oh, yes, but I can't say the same thing for you. I've been watching you. I'd say you were more on edge than anything. Why,

I wonder?"

"It's just that I'm not at my best in these surroundings," Kessie said. "I'm not a water creature, unfortunately."

"I wouldn't say that," Jonathon smiled. "You were doing all right with our blonde giant friend before Andrea butted in."

Kessie knew her colour was rising. "I work for Brent's father," she said, "and that's the beginning and end of my relationship with Brent."

"He was more than a little interested in you," Jonathon remarked "and I can't say I blame him."

Kessie smiled. "Let's talk about you," she said. "How do you enjoy your work? Is Andrea very famous?"

Jonathon shrugged. "Not really, she's trying to make her way up the ladder at the moment." He shook his head. "I like her a lot, but she isn't very successful, I'm afraid, though anyone can see she's good to look at."

"That's not very loyal," Kessie protested, feeling suddenly sorry for Andrea.

"Maybe not," Jonathon said, "but you did ask and I think you're the type who respects honesty. Don't worry about Andrea, she'll make out, she'll always earn plenty of money from advertising if nothing else."

Just then, Andrea came out of the water dripping wet, her hair spread round her shoulders like a dark cloak. Beside her, Brent looked very tall and muscular, and Kessie found it hard to take her eyes from him as the couple approached.

"Jonathon!" Andrea said smiling. "I see you've already made the acquaintance of our little manageress." She smiled at Kessie. "Don't allow him to take you in with his flattery, my dear girl, he could charm the birds from the trees, that's one reason why he works for me."

She introduced the two men to each other and they eyed each other warily. Kessie had the feeling they were each weighing the other up as a potential rival.

Andrea stood between the two of them, turning her shoulder and somehow managing the exclude Kessie from the company.

"I think I'll go and change," Kessie murmured, and then Andrea gave her a glance over her shoulder.

"Go on dear," she said. "Don't bother about us, we'll be fine."

Brent moved from the small group and stood beside Kessie, towering above her.

"Are you sure you've had enough of swimming lessons?" he asked, and Kessie smiled at him a little uncomfortably.

"Yes, I'll call it a day for now," she said. "Perhaps some other time?" She was surprised at the coolness of her voice, which was at complete variance with the tumult of emotion seething inside her. She wanted to put her arms around Brent's neck, draw him to her and beg him to kiss her.

She looked away from him sharply and was just about to move away when the wall telephone began to ring.

"Excuse me," she said, pleased to be provided with an excuse for leaving. "I expect that's for me."

The desk clerk sounded agitated. "There are dozens of newspaper men here, Miss

Danton," he said. "They're coming in the direction of the pool, I'm afraid I couldn't stop them. They said that a Jonathon Finch had invited them."

Kessie turned and looked at Andrea. She was laughing, her head flung back, her hair swinging. So this was what she'd meant by not having to pay out a penny herself for the party. She was hoping that the publicity would cover the costs. Kessie was suddenly very angry.

"Why didn't you let me know there were reporters coming to the party?" She looked from Andrea to Jonathon and then at Brent.

"They are on the way here at this very moment," she said. "I'd have liked to have been prepared."

"Don't worry," Jonathon said smoothly, "it's all good publicity for the hotel too, you know, and free at that."

Kessie looked around her at the guests in swimming costumes lying around the pool. The scene was more one of some remains of a Roman banquet than a picture of a select hotel.

"You must send them away," Kessie said. "I won't have them taking photographs in here." It was too late, the doors swung open and about half a dozen reporters with cameras slung around their necks stood grinning around them.

Kessie blinked as a flashbulb went off and then she was aware of Jonathon with his arm around her waist, drawing her close to him.

"Come along fellas!" he called. "Get one of the pretty little manageress."

Again Kessie's eyes were blinded by the flash and then she was aware that Brent was coming forward, an angry look on his face. He caught Jonathon by the shoulder and spun him around.

"That's enough!" he said. "Now get out of here."

There was a scuffle and then Brent placed a blow firmly on Jonathon's jaw as lights flashed and someone screamed. Then Kessie felt herself being pushed. The water swung below her for a terrible few seconds before she hit it and felt it close, suffocatingly, over her head.

FIVE

When Kessie woke the next morning, her head ached and her eyes were puffy as though she'd been weeping. She sneezed violently and sighed in exasperation. It was no wonder she'd caught a cold, she'd stood for what seemed hours after Brent had fished her out of the pool, trying to sort out the confusion that had raged with Jonathon Finch threatening to sue Brent and the hotel and it appeared everyone else in sight.

She pulled on a robe and swallowed a few aspirins before going to stand in front of the mirror. She looked awful, her hair hanging in limp strands around her white face and her nose was red and shiny.

There was a knock on the door and before

she could even call an answer it was opened and Brent strode into the room.

"If I were you I'd get straight back into bed, you look terrible," he said bluntly.

"Thanks!" Kessie's voice was heavy with sarcasm and she turned her back on him unable to bear the look of amusement in his face.

"I'm all right!" she insisted, but her throat felt raw and she was aware of Brent's disbelief.

"It sounds like it. Stay in bed for today, I insist, I'll be around to see that everything runs smoothly.

Kessie climbed on the bed, surprised to find that she did feel a little weak.

"I'll get someone to bring you up a cup of tea," he said and moved towards the door. "It would be just as well to get a doctor too."

"No!" Kessie said, but she was too late. Brent had gone, closing the door behind him. She sighed and leaned against the pillows. He was a stubborn man all right, and yet she couldn't help the sense of elation that filled her as she thought of

Brent's anger when Jonathon Finch had put his arm around her.

One of the chambermaids brought in a tray of tea and handed a folded newspaper to Kessie.

"You in it, Miss Danton," the girl said in halting English. "It is a very good picture."

With swiftly beating heart, Kessie unfolded the newspaper and saw with a gasp of horror that a whole page had been devoted to the scuffle at the poolside. There was a picture of herself apparently in an embrace with Jonathon Finch and then another of Brent landing a punch on the man's jaw.

"Oh, good heavens!" Kessie said, "are these pictures in all the papers?"

"I expect so," the girl said with a broad grin, and she went out, chuckling to herself.

Kessie jumped out of bed. She would get dressed, have a quick cup of tea and go and find Brent. It was a certainty that if Lars saw these pictures he'd soon come hotfooting it back.

She poured herself a cup of tea and drank it quickly. It eased her throat a little, but just as she was about to leave the room, the doctor, with Brent at his side, was on his way to see her.

"Up and about already, young lady?" The doctor put down his case and smiled. "I knew you were a sturdy one, didn't I tell you not to worry?" He looked at Brent and Kessie bit her lip, wondering what was behind the doctor's smile. Had he seen the newspapers too?

"I'm all right," she said. "Just a little sore throat, nothing to worry about, really."

"I'll give you a spray for that," the doctor said. "Let's just have a look at you. Will you wait outside please, Mr Tolkelarson?"

Kessie was in a fever of impatience as the doctor insisted on giving her a thorough examination. He listened to her chest and nodded in satisfaction.

"Very good, now I can truly tell your young man that there's nothing wrong with you, young lady, except a bad cold. "

Kessie didn't try to explain, it was too complicated, but once the doctor left, she called Brent to her room.

"You've seen the papers?" she said. "What's Lars going to think, and perhaps most important, what will Inga believe when she reads of you apparently brawling over me?"

Brent smiled, his grey eyes difficult to read. "I shouldn't let it worry you, I can cope with Inga. As for my father, he will just have to accept my explanation. I shouldn't think he'd blame you, Kessie.

"But I am to blame," she said. "I shouldn't have been so gullible. I might have known that Andrea had something up her sleeves. She was practically telling me so only I was too stupid to listen."

"Well, there's no point going over it now," Brent said, putting his hands on her shoulders. "You're not supposed to talk, remember?"

"But," Kessie began, and then Brent's lips were on hers, gently at first and then warming with passion. He drew her close and she couldn't help the way her arms wound around his neck. How she loved him. It was all she could do not to tell him exactly how she felt about him.

It was he who drew away first, he seemed as shaken as she was. They stared at each other in silence for a moment and then just as he was about to speak, there was a loud knocking on the door.

"I'll go." He moved away from her and suddenly Kessie felt cold. She heard the murmur of voices in the passage and then Brent came back into the room.

"There's been a phone call from my father," he said. "It seems he's chartering an aeroplane and flying in to the Sornefjord. He wants an explanation of the newspaper stories."

"I knew he'd be furious," Kessie said. "How long will it take him to get here?"

"An hour," Brent said, "no more, but don't look so frightened, I won't let him eat you."

Kessie looked up at Brent suddenly. "Has Lars got a pilot's licence then?" she said, and Brent looked at her in amusement.

"Yes, and so have I. What's that got to do with anything?"

Kessie smiled. "Why have none of you thought of flying guests to the hotel by helicopter?" she said. "It would be an added attraction, surely?"

Brent nodded thoughtfully. "Yes I suppose it would work, especially when the weather was good in the summer months. It could be too dangerous in the deep of winter, however."

"Well," Kessie shrugged, "I shouldn't think there'd be all that many guests in the depths of winter anyway. Why not put the idea to Lars?"

"You put it," Brent said, "it's your idea and it might just take his mind off the newspaper stories."

Kessie smiled. "All right, I will." She crossed her fingers. "Let's hope that he's simmered down by the time he gets here."

Her hope was a false one. Lars came into the hotel, his face dark, a stack of newspapers under his arm.

"Kessie, I wish to speak to you in the office at once," he said. Brent winked at her but Kessie was trembling. She knew that

113

Lars' anger was justified. She scarcely looked at Eric who was following his father along the corridor.

"Can you explain this?" Lars tapped the papers with a forefinger, his voice full of contained anger.

"I'm sorry," Kessie said weakly. "It was a contingency I hadn't prepared for when I agreed to Andrea Davidson's holding a party here."

Brent leaned against the closed door. He gave Kessie a reassuring smile.

"It was just as much my fault," he said. "Neither of us had anticipated a gang of pressmen gate-crashing the way they did."

"And was Kessie forced into wearing that skimpy bathing suit and were you bound to end up brawling?" He banged a fist on the desk. "It seems I cannot trust you to carry out even the simplest of tasks with any sort of efficiency."

"Look, father," Brent said mildly, "I know the newspapers have gone to town on the story but it's been blown up out of all pro-portion."

"It looks as though there was some sort of orgy going on at the hotel, Brent, and I will not have that sort of thing." He glanced at Kessie.

"I expected better of you than this. If only your father were alive, he'd know how to deal with you."

A light tap on the door interrupted Lars and he shook his head angrily.

"Send them away, whoever it is," he said shortly to Brent, but the door swung open and Andrea stood looking around the room, a brilliant smile on her face, her long hair lifted up in an elegant chignon.

"Oh, please excuse me for interrupting you," she said sweetly. "I can see that you're all very busy, but I simply had to come and apologise for the way the reporters acted. They were totally irresponsible, the way they handled the story. It's a lot of silly nonsense and I just hope everyone has the good sense to treat it as such."

She moved towards Lars, holding out her hand. "I'm Andrea Davidson," she said, "and I know who you are, I've read about

115

you in the newspapers. Had quite a lot of publicity yourself from time to time, haven't you, and not all of it good!"

Lars looked a little abashed. "Well, it's true these reporters sometimes exaggerate or even invent situations," he said slowly.

"Of course!" Andrea said, smiling into Lars' eyes. "I do wish you'd come and have a cup of coffee with me and allow me to make amends in some way for all the bother I've caused."

Lars seemed bemused. "Yes, that would be very nice," he said, looking around him. "Well, what are you all waiting for, there's work to be done."

Kessie made her way quickly to her room and sat on the bed, her hands shaking. She'd half expected Lars to dismiss her there and then, but it seemed Andrea had saved the day.

There was a knock on the door and Brent looked in, smiling at her.

"It wasn't so bad, was it?" He came further into the room and looked at her in concern.

"You're very pale, Kessie, are you feeling all right?" He caught her chin in his hand gently and stared down at her.

"Yes, I'm fine," she said. "It was lucky for us that Andrea came in when she did, though, I thought I was going to be told to pack my things."

"No," Brent shook his head, "I don't think my father would go to those lengths, he is very fond of you and feels that he has to care for you. I think I can understand that better now."

She couldn't meet his eyes. She felt him make a move towards her and before she could turn away, his lips were touching hers, gently, searchingly. She ached to cling to him, to bury her face in his shoulder, but that was impossible.

"Aren't you forgetting something?" she asked, drawing away from him. "You're engaged to Inga."

"No," he said, "I hadn't forgotten. Come here, Kessie, you know you like to be in my arms. Do you deny it?"

"I don't deny there's a physical attraction,

no," she said, trying desperately to control her emotions. "But surely we are adult enough to recognise that for the shallow instinct that it is?"

His arms fell away from her. "I see." He moved to the door and turned to look at her briefly. "Well I shan't bother you again with my animal desires, don't you worry."

As the door closed behind him, Kessie almost called his name. But what good would that do? It wouldn't change the fact that he wasn't free.

She rubbed her face with her hands. She felt suddenly very tired. She was not doing very well here in Norway. She wasn't even successful at her job. Perhaps she should just give up now and go home to London. She toyed with the idea for a few minutes but deep within her she knew she wouldn't leave, at least not yet. She had to prove to herself if to no one else that she was capable of carrying out the responsible job Lars had given her.

As the days went slowly by, Lars became more friendly and Kessie knew it was

Andrea's doing. She was almost constantly with Lars, talking animatedly to him, while he seemed content to look at her and admire her.

"Could I have a word with you, Lars?" Kessie asked as he sat in the sunlounge at Andrea's side. She smiled apologetically. "I promise I won't keep you long."

"Sit here." Lars indicated the lounger at his side. "Relax a little, every time I see you there's a tense worried look on your face."

He caught her hand. "I'm sorry if I've been a bit grim my dear, I didn't mean it, I was just annoyed with all the publicity, that's all."

"I realise that," Kessie said, "but as it's turned out there has been a load of mail requesting information about the Sornefjord."

She sat down and Andrea smiled at her over Lars's shoulder. She seemed happy and content and Kessie wondered if she ever did any work at all these days.

"I was wondering if it would be a good idea to use a helicopter to bring guests up from the valley," Kessie said. "I know you have your licence and so has Brent, and I think it would be an extra advantage if the hotel offered such a service."

"I do agree!" Andrea leaned forward eagerly. "That's a wonderful idea." She looked up at Lars wide-eyed, "I didn't know you could fly until I saw your arrival here. You're a wonderful man, Lars."

Kessie glanced quickly at Andrea, wondering if she was laying on the flattery a bit too thickly but she seemed genuinely enchanted by him.

Lars smiled. "Yes, I'm sure it's a very good idea. I don't know why I hadn't thought of it myself."

Andrea leaned forward, her eyes alight with admiration, her small hand just touching his sleeve.

"You can't think of everything, Lars, that's why you're so clever in employing someone like Kessie."

Lars nodded. "Yes, I'm fortunate in my choice of manageress, I do agree with you there."

He reached into his pocket and drew out some papers, holding them out to Kessie. "Here are some of the costings I've had worked out. Take a look at them. See how high the price of feeding the horses comes and then there's the stabling and grooming. It's quite a sizeable amount of money there."

Kessie nodded thoughtfully. "Yes, I agree and perhaps you might be able to offset the expense of the helicopter by cutting down on the amount of animals you keep. Some of them will have to stay, of course. I don't think it would be a good idea to dispense with the use of the horses altogether."

"I agree." Lars got to his feet. "I'll begin making some enquiries right away. I'm quite excited about the prospect of acquiring a helicopter for the hotel."

"Oh don't go, Lars." Andrea pouted up at him. "I shall miss you dreadfully."

Lars smiled. "I promise I won't be long, and in the meantime Kessie can stay and talk to you."

"Well," Andrea lay back against the

lounger, "I must say that as far as I'm concerned Lars is the best man I've met for ages. He's so mature and kind, I'm sick of young men who only want me because they think I can further their career."

Kessie was at a loss. "You seem to get along very well," she said, "and you certainly calmed him down over the business of the photographers."

"Well, dear, it was all my fault, really, I just hadn't given it a thought. I mean, I didn't expect the party to be portrayed as a sort of wild happening. And I didn't know Lars then or I might have handled things differently." She sat up in her chair, looking over Kessie's shoulder.

"Oh, dear, here comes trouble," she said in a low voice and Kessie turned in time to see Jonathon Finch coming towards them.

"So you're still here, taking things easy?" he began, his tone ominous. "Do you know I've had to turn down at least four jobs for you already. I can't go on making excuses. Soon you'll be forgotten, and how will you feel then?"

Andrea looked down at her hands. "I don't know, but then what have I ever done that was so memorable anyway? Who cares about soap powder or toothpaste ads?"

"It's all bread and butter," Jonathon said quickly, and Andrea flung back her dark hair.

"Yours as well as mine," she said caustically. She closed her eyes. "Please Jonathon, leave me alone, I need a rest, can't you see that?"

"Come on, Andrea." Jonathon leaned over her, grasping her shoulder. "You should be cashing in on all that publicity I arranged for the party."

"So that was your doing?" Lars had come up quietly and was watching the proceedings with inscrutable eyes, and for the first time, Kessie noticed how alike Brent and his father were.

Jonathon Finch got to his feet. "Yes, want to make something of it?" he said belligerently.

"Jonathon, for heaven's sake!" Andrea pulled at his arm. "This is Mr. Tolkelarson, the hotel owner."

"Oh, I see." Jonathon seemed to lose all his pomp. "Well, then I suppose I spoke out of turn. I apologise."

"That is all right," Lars said, "but perhaps you would be so kind as to leave my hotel now?"

Jonathon began to bluster and Lars moved a step nearer. Andrea just lay where she was, staring at the two men in apparent confusion.

"I'm going." He turned to Andrea. "But as an actress you're finished, do you understand, you'll get no work if I can help it, ever!"

He walked away and Andrea sighed. "Oh, dear, I think he's upset."

Kessie pushed down the desire to laugh. Andrea's gift for understatement was incredible.

Lars sat beside Andrea, his face full of concern. "Was that man important to your career?" he said. "If so I will call him back at once."

"No," Andrea shook her head, "don't do

that, Lars. My so-called career just isn't worth the candle."

She leaned forward and touched Lars' cheek. "Do you know," she said, "I've never had anyone stand up for me like that, I'm so thrilled!"

Kessie, unnoticed, got quietly to her feet and walked swiftly away. Why couldn't she be so open with Brent, she wondered miserably, but then Brent was engaged to another woman, and in any case he didn't show her the open admiration that Lars bestowed so readily on Andrea.

"Kessie." Eric was standing before her, a smile on his face. "Wake up, I've spoken to you twice and you haven't heard me. You're far away."

"Oh, I'm sorry, Eric." Kessie made an effort to smile. She hadn't really spoken a great deal to Eric since he and his father had returned from the city, and she wasn't sure what sort of mood he was in.

He put an arm around her shoulder. "Don't look so woebegone, I'm not going to eat you."

"Don't be silly, Eric." She laughed. "I just wondered if you were annoyed about the publicity. Your father was pretty mad and I don't blame him."

Eric grinned. "I was too busy looking at the pictures of you in a bikini to be mad," he said, and Kessie felt a prickle of embarrassment colour her face.

"Oh, don't mention that," she said flatly, "I don't know what on earth possessed me to wear the stupid thing in the first place!"

It was dim in the corridor and Eric stopped walking, turning Kessie round to face him.

"But you looked beautiful," he said softly, "really beautiful. I only wish I'd been here to see you in person."

She tried to move away but Eric held her firmly. "Please Eric, I've work to do," she said and he smiled.

"So conscientious all of a sudden? Come along, don't be afraid of me, I'm not going to hurt you."

"But you are hurting me," Kessie said as calmly as she could. "Let my arm go please."

He caught her round the waist and drew her close to him, and Kessie sighed in exasperation.

"Eric, this is foolish, let me go." She pushed against him but he had no intention of releasing her.

"I'll let you go if you give me one kiss," he said. "Is that much to ask, one little kiss?"

"No, Eric, someone might come along here any minute," Kessie protested, "and how do you think that would look? Aren't I in enough trouble with your father as it is?"

"I'm serious about you, Kessie," Eric said, "I want to marry you."

She gasped. "But that's absurd! You hardly know me." She tried again to push him away but he held her fast.

"Listen Kessie, how long do you think you have to know a person?"

He was right, she'd only known Brent a short while and yet she was in love with him. But still, Eric was a young man, a little impulsive and silly. He didn't really mean what he was saying.

"It's no good," she said, deciding to tell

him the truth, at least some of it. "I'm already in love with someone else."

"You can't be!" Eric held her at arm's length, staring into her face. "You haven't had a chance to go out with anyone since you came her. Unless," his face darkened, "you're in love with Brent. That's it, that's what you're trying to tell me!"

Kessie shook her head in despair. "Don't jump to conclusions, Eric. How do you know it's not someone I left behind in London, a man who isn't free to love me in return?"

He seemed uncertain, and Kessie pressed home her advantage.

"You don't really know much about me at all, do you, Eric? You only think you're in love with me."

"Don't treat me like a child!" he said savagely, and Kessie realised too late that she'd said the wrong thing.

"I didn't mean it to sound like that," she said quickly, but Eric wasn't listening, he was hurrying her along the corridor and up the small back staircase.

"Eric, let me go at once!" she said, suddenly frightened. "Where do you think you're taking me?"

"Somewhere we can be alone," he said, "I'm taking you to my room, I'll show you if I'm a man or not."

"Eric, this is silly, please calm down!" Kessie's voice was rising and she tried to take a deep breath, to fight the feeling of panic that was threatening to overwhelm her.

He took no notice of her struggles and almost propelled her into his room, closing the door after them with a violent bang.

"Eric, this has gone far enough." Kessie tried to be very much on her dignity, but her hair was tangled over her face and she was trembling.

"I love you, Kessie!" Eric said, and pulled her towards him, imprisoning her in his arms.

"I don't love you!" Kessie said. "Now let me go at once before I start to scream and make a fool of us both!"

He pressed his mouth down on hers, and

Kessie twisted away from him.

"You are only making things worse by turning away from me," Eric said savagely. "You are doing this to tease me, aren't you?"

"No!" Kessie almost shouted the word, and then suddenly the door opened and Brent stood there, his face darkening as he took in the scene before him. In two strides he was across the room, dragging Eric from Kessie.

"Please!" she said, "don't fight, I couldn't bear it." She stood against the wall shivering as the two men faced each other.

"What in heaven's name do you think you're doing?" Brent asked, shaking Eric as though he was a child.

"I have as much right to ask Kessie to marry me as the next man!" Eric said. "At least my intentions are honourable and that can't be said of yours, dear brother. I didn't spend the night alone with her, but you did. And then you appear in the paper brawling over her. What is anyone supposed to think?"

"Anyone can think what he likes," Brent

said in a deceptively calm voice, "but let anyone so much as speak his thoughts aloud and I'll be there to reckon with him. Now are you going to say anything or not?"

Eric shook his head. "I know you could knock me down," he said, "but that doesn't prove anything except perhaps that you have a guilty conscience."

"Please!" Kessie said, "don't quarrel any more. I'm leaving the hotel tomorrow, I've brought nothing but trouble since I came here and now you two are going to fight and I can't bear it."

She dragged open the door and ran from the room, not wanting to hear any more. She just wanted to get to her own room where she could shut herself in and be alone.

Fortunately, she met no one along the corridors and with a sigh of relief, she locked her door and then flung herself down on the bed.

She put her hands up to her hot cheeks. Her heart was beating so rapidly that she could hardly breathe. She'd been a fool ever to have left London and all that was familiar to her. She'd been an even bigger fool to fall in love with Brent. The sooner she cut her losses and left the Sornefjord for good the better.

SIX

Kessie's resolution to give in her notice to Lars came to nothing after all. He sent for her and once she was with him in the office she felt carried away by his enthusiasm for the new project he had in mind.

"A health spa," he said like a magician producing a rabbit from a hat. "A simple wooden building behind the hotel with a sauna and perhaps some keep-fit apparatus, don't you think it will add to the facilities of the hotel?"

"Yes," Kessie said, "I can see that it would, but will it take long?"

Lars shook his head. "No, not with local workers. And you have to admit there is plenty of wood up here, enough to build a hundred of the cabins that I have in mind."

"Well it seems a fine idea," Kessie said. "I shouldn't think it would cost much."

"No," Lars agreed. "And with the addition of a helicopter to bring up the guests if the weather is bad, I can see that business will be booming." He smiled. "I'm starting lessons in flying the damned machine this afternoon as a matter of fact."

Kessie could see that he was as excited as a small boy at the prospect.

He glanced at his watch. "I do believe it's time for lunch, my dear. Never let it be said I'm a tyrant to work for, off you go and get something to eat."

Kessie smiled. It was good to see Lars in a happy frame of mind, he seemed to have forgotten entirely his disapproval of the party and the resulting publicity.

"I'll see you later, Lars," she said as she left the office. Come to think of it, she needed some lunch, she felt quite hungry.

Her feet sank into the soft pile of the carpet as she crossed the reception hall on her way to the restaurant. She took a deep breath as she saw Brent coming towards her. She had kept out of his way since the quarrel he'd had with Eric and now she was unable to meet his eyes.

"Hello!" She forced a bright note into her voice. "Lars has just been telling me about his new idea for a sauna spa. It's an excellent one, don't you think?"

"I wouldn't know," Brent said, "he hasn't yet confided in me. Now if you'll excuse me, I'm rather busy."

"Wait!" She caught his arm. "Brent, I'm sorry about what happened with Eric. Whatever you might think of me, you can't believe I encouraged him at all."

"No?" Brent's eyes were cold and hard. "That's not what he told me. In fact he told me quite a few things of interest after you'd gone, about this man you have back in London for instance. I suppose you think it's fun to amuse yourself while you're here waiting for the time when you can go back to him."

He began to walk away and Kessie hurried after him. She clung to his sleeve but he walked on as though unaware of her. With hot cheeks she watched him go. How could he believe all that nonsense? Couldn't he guess she'd only told Eric those lies to put him off?

She carried on walking towards the restaurant although her appetite seemed to have suddenly disappeared.

"Kessie!" Andrea was waving to her from the corner of the room, sitting at what seemed to have become her own table.

"Kessie, come and join me!" Andrea wasn't easily ignored and reluctantly Kessie made her way across the room. The last thing she felt like at the moment was company but she couldn't be downright rude.

Sunlight spilled in from the large window and the view outside was breathtaking.

"You're looking awful," Andrea said bluntly, "what on earth's wrong?"

"Nothing, really," Kessie said quickly, "I suppose I was just deep in thought."

"Come along and sit down. Have your lunch with me, I hate being alone. Lars said he would join me later but goodness knows when that will be."

"You seem to be getting on very well with Lars." Kessie was quick to change the conversation from herself, and Andrea's face lit up.

"He's wonderful, I can't imagine what my life was like without him. The best thing in the world happened to me when I came here, believe me."

"He's a fine man," Kessie agreed. "He was always very kind to me when he came to stay with us at our London hotel."

"You have a hotel in London?" Andrea asked in surprise and Kessie smiled.

"Used to have," she said. "When my father died, Lars bought the Danton from me and gave me this job here. I would have been lost without him."

"Well at least you have money in the bank and can be independent," Andrea said. "I never know where my next penny is coming from."

She looked over Kessie's shoulder. "Here comes Eric," she said. "I'm sure the boy's in love with you, he can't take his eyes off you."

Kessie's heart sank as Eric sat beside her, a smile on his face. He acted as though nothing untoward had happened between them.

"How nice to have the pleasure of two lovely ladies at lunch time," he said with a smile. "You don't mind if I join you, I hope?"

"Of course not!" It was Andrea who answered him. "Perhaps you can tell me what wine I should have with this lovely Norwegian dish I've ordered."

They talked together for a few minutes and Kessie sat back in her chair, wishing she was anywhere but here in Norway. She felt she just couldn't cope with all that was happening.

"And what about you, Kessie?" Eric leaned towards her, his eyes staring directly into hers. She looked away quickly. "What are you going to have to eat?" Eric continued.

"Something light," Kessie said, "I'm not really very hungry. What do you suggest, Eric?"

Andrea leaned forward. "I do believe the girl's in love!" she said with a smile. "She wanders around the place lost in a dream and now she says she's off her food. Definite symptoms, I'd say!"

"Who are you in love with Kessie?" Eric asked, and there was a hint of anger in his voice.

Andrea interrupted again. "At a guess I'd say she's in love with Brent, your brother. Isn't that right, Kessie?"

She knew her colour was rising but Kessie made an attempt to answer normally.

"Of course not, I hardly know him." She saw Eric's eyes flicker over her in speculation.

"Well," he said, "I don't think Brent is aware of anyone but Inga, so you've no chance there, Kessie." He leaned forward and put his arm around her shoulder. "Wouldn't I do instead?"

Andrea laughed. "I think you make a very attractive couple, she said, "why not take him up on his offer, Kessie?"

"I don't know why you two are talking

such rubbish!" Kessie said. "I'm not in love with anyone and I don't intend to be, at least not while I'm here at the Sornefjord, so let's allow the subject to die a natural death, shall we?"

"Saving yourself for your boyfriend in London, are you?" Eric said sarcastically. "Does he know about your little episode with Brent?"

Kessie rose to her feet. "Please excuse me," she said. "I don't think I'll stay for lunch after all. I'm not really hungry and I find it so hot in here."

"Oh, don't go," Andrea said in contrition. "We're only teasing you, aren't we, Eric? Tell her she must stay."

"No really." Kessie moved away. "I'll see you later on, perhaps."

She made her way towards the office and opened the door quickly. It was only when she was inside that she saw Brent sitting behind the desk, the telephone in his hand.

"I'm sorry," she said, "I didn't mean to intrude." She would have left but he waved his hand to her indicating that she stay.

She watched him replace the receiver and then he looked directly at her, his eyes meeting hers, unreadable in their darkness.

"That was Inga," he said after a moment. "She wanted to let me know that our engagement is at an end."

"Oh, I'm sorry." Kessie stumbled over the words, ashamed of the sudden feeling of gladness that flared inside her.

"Are you sorry, really?" Brent asked, and as he rose from the desk and came towards her, Kessie didn't know whether she should face him or run away. There was a look in his eye that almost frightened her.

"What can I say?" she appealed to him. "Did Inga give you any reason for breaking off the engagement?"

"She did as a matter of fact." Brent looked at her. "She said she couldn't compete against you."

The colour flared into Kessie's cheeks just as Brent reached and drew her towards him. His mouth came down on hers hard and fierce. She couldn't help but respond and her arms crept around his shoulders.

She longed to tell him that she loved him, that she would gladly take Inga's place, but then he was holding her away from him, staring down at her with hot anger in his eyes.

"That's just what you want, isn't it?" he said. "Another conquest. You seem to enjoy making a fool of anyone who pays you a little attention."

"Brent!" she drew back against the door, leaning against it for support. "I don't want to make a fool of you or anyone else!"

"What about that poor sucker in London who thinks you're patiently waiting for him to get his freedom?"

"Listen to me, Brent," Kessie said desperately. "He doesn't exist, I invented him just to put Eric off."

"You expect me to believe that?" He pulled her away from the door. "You tell so many lies you don't even recognise the truth any longer. Why did you have to come here in the first place?"

Kessie clasped her hands together to stop them from trembling. She swallowed hard and tried to control her voice.

"You know why I came here," she said, "it was as a favour to your father. He wanted me to take over his new hotel. It was as simple as that."

"A favour to my father!" Brent said. "That's almost funny."

"Will you explain what you're getting at?" Kessie said in desperation. "Tell me what it is you have against me? You were hostile from the first moment I arrived in Norway. Isn't it about time you told me why?"

The door opened suddenly and Lars came into the office, giving Kessie and Brent a quick glance. If he saw there was anything amiss, he chose to ignore the fact.

"Ah, good, now that you are both here, we can discuss a few points about the new plans." He said down behind the desk and looked up, waiting for them to comply.

"I'm rather busy, father," Brent said quietly, but his father waved his protest aside.

"Nonsense, nothing could be more important than this, sit down and listen to me for five minutes."

Kessie was the first to obey, and then with a shrug Brent sat down at her side, his arm brushing hers. In spite of all that had passed between them in the last five minutes she could not help feeling a thrill of pleasure at his nearness.

"I have seen about the purchase of a helicopter," Lars said, smiling expansively, "and I think we shall need a regular pilot as well as taking charge of a few trips ourselves."

"Very well, Father, if that's what you've decided," Brent said. "It's your business after all."

"Come don't be churlish, Brent," Lars smiled. "After all it affects you as well as me." He paused. "I want you to see about the advertising of the latest facilities, the sauna spa and the further attractions of the flight here by helicopter."

Brent nodded. "Yes, I'll do that, but I hope you've thought out the finances of the scheme very carefully. You've already sustained a financial loss that you've yet to make up."

"Nonsense!" Lars said genially. "One loss is neither here nor there, and in any case I still have a few plans in that direction which I'll talk about when I've more time." He glanced at his watch.

"What loss?" Kessie asked in bewilderment. "The hotel is always booked solid. I don't see how it could make a loss."

"Brent is talking about another little venture of mine, dear," Lars said quickly. "He is too cautious. I haven't built up a chain of hotels by practising caution, I can tell you that!"

"I agree with Lars," Kessie said, at a loss to understand Brent's attitude. "You have to expand the business if you possibly can, otherwise there's never any progress."

"And you are of course an astute businesswoman, Kessie, I'll grant you that much."

"Come along," Lars said, rising from behind his desk. "I must go. As for you two, why not have a cup of tea together, or go for a walk in the beautiful sunshine? Make the most of it, because once the height of the season is here there won't be very much spare time for anyone."

"Shall we take Lars' advise and go for a walk?" Kessie found herself saying. "Perhaps we could iron a few things out."

"You're wasting your time," Brent said, staring down at her. "You're backing my father all the way along the line, aren't you, and not even considering if there's enough money for these little details."

"Surely there's no lack of money?" Kessie asked in surprise, and Brent smiled with no amusement in his face.

"My father threw away a good deal of money when he bought the Danton, but then of course you must know that."

"I do not know any such thing!" Kessie said hotly. "The Danton is a good hotel."

"It was before the council had the bright idea to allow a bigger, more modern hotel to be built almost next door. Now the thing's losing money hand over fist. It's hardly worth keeping the place open."

Kessie bit her lip. "I knew nothing of this. Your father bought the hotel from me before I was even over the shock of my father's death."

"Do you expect me to believe that?" Brent said flatly. "Even if you are speaking the truth, you don't have to keep prodding my father to spend yet more money on schemes that may come to nothing."

"But the idea of the sauna spa was his own," she protested, "and as for the helicopter idea, can't you see how much pleasure it's bringing him? Why, he takes lessons every day."

"And you can't even begin to guess how much they are costing, can you?"

He walked away and Kessie watched him, unable to say anything.

What a mess. She made her way upstairs and along the corridor to her room. She had to be alone, to think things out. There must be something she could do to put things right.

Perhaps she could give Lars the money back. But would he accept it? She doubted that very much. May she could persuade him to let her put some money into the Sornefjord. Wouldn't that help?

At all costs, she mustn't let Lars know Brent had told her what had happened over the Danton. He would be furious with his son and she'd caused enough trouble among the family as it was.

She sat on her bed and closed her eyes. Only then she remembered that Brent's engagement to Inga was over. It seemed that she, Kessie, was somehow to blame for that too. She was a jinx on the hotel and the people in it, and she still hadn't given up her idea of leaving and returning to London. A little voice inside her told her not to be a fool. She loved Brent, she must stay and somehow convince him that she wasn't the little cheat he imagined her to be.

It was difficult working with Lars and not blurting out that she knew how far his kindness had taken him. She felt guilty every time she thought of him paying her for the Danton and then finding he'd been landed with a dud deal.

Brent seemed to be keeping out of her way, and when she did see him, she inadvertently walked in on an argument he was having with his father.

"I will not accept your resignation, Brent," Lars was saying, thumping his desk to emphasise his words. "I need you here with me, you know that."

"No, father," Brent shook his head. "You have plenty of assistance without me, it's time I made my own way in the world."

"You haven't very much money, Brent, except for what your mother left you and the small amount you've invested here. That's not going to give you much of a start."

"I don't know," Brent said quickly. "You yourself started off with much less than that, didn't you?"

Lars sighed. "Can't you persuade him to stay, Kessie? The boy doesn't realise how much I depend on him."

Kessie shook her head dumbly. There was nothing she could say that would change Brent's mind, but if he left the Sornefjord she didn't think she could bear it without him.

"Very well," Lars said heavily. "Go if you

must, but first, please do the advertising of the spa for me, will you?"

"Yes," Brent said flatly, "I'll do that. What sort of advertising did you have in mind?"

"Well you and Eric can go round my chain of hotels and put up notices. At least it won't be a dull job, you must see that."

Kessie stared at Brent. How could he think of going away, didn't he feel anything at all for her?

"I'll leave as soon as possible," Brent was saying, and Lars inclined his head.

"Very well, you can start off first thing in the morning. Is that soon enough for you? Oh, find Eric, will you Brent, and tell him about the change of plan."

Brent nodded and moved to the door. "Thank you for at least trying to understand, Father," he said.

He walked past Kessie as though he hadn't even seen her and she stared at Lars, unable to hide her dismay.

"What's wrong, child?" Lars said in concern. "You're as white as a sheet. Sit down I'll give you a little brandy."

Kessie stared at him. "No, I'm all right, thank you Lars, I'm not really ill, really I'm not."

"What is it then?" Lars was insistent. "I can see that something is wrong."

Suddenly, Kessie knew she had to tell him the truth, the time for platitudes was past.

"I'm in love with Brent," she said bluntly, and it was a relief to speak her feelings out loud. Lars stared at her for a long time in silence.

"And Brent, does he care for you in return?" he asked slowly, sitting down on the edge of the desk and folding his arms across his chest.

"Oh, no," she said, "he's just made that abundantly clear. He can't get away from me quickly enough."

"Brent is a difficult man to know," Lars said quietly, "he doesn't easily reveal his true feelings."

"I've found out how difficult he is to know!" Kessie said feelingly. "Sometimes, I think he must care a little, but then he couldn't just walk away from me if there was one crumb of liking there for me, could he?"

"He's my son," Lars said, "but he's a grown man and I can't read his mind any more than you can. Why don't you just ask him outright if he cares?"

"I dare not!" Kessie said, "I don't think I'm strong enough to face the answer. Lars, should I leave Norway for good?"

"I do not wish that to happen, my dear," Lars said, "but you have to make up your own mind about this."

"Lars," Kessie said slowly, "there is one more thing I must talk to you about. The Danton."

"No more!" Lars waved a hand at her impatiently. "Go now and leave me in peace, I have enough to think about as it is without your continuing to question me."

He waved her away. "Go now, leave me, I have to concentrate on these estimates."

"No, Lars," Kessie stood firm. "I must know the truth. Is the Danton draining your resources, are you sustaining a loss because of it?"

Lars sighed. "Someone has been talking

too much!" he said. "All right, yes, the Danton has been a liability." He held up his hand, stopping her when she would have spoken.

"The land, however, has great value, and if I sell the Danton, as I plan to, then I shall recoup my losses."

He smiled sympathetically at her. "Leave it now, don't worry your pretty little head about it, things will work out, you'll see."

In a daze, Kessie left the office. She couldn't believe that the Danton was to be sold only to be demolished. It had been her home since childhood and it was difficult to believe it would soon be no more.

Suddenly, she hit on a brilliant solution. She would buy the Danton herself with the money Lars had paid her for the hotel when her father died. She wouldn't allow Lars to know about her plan, he was sure to try to put her off and he might even stipulate that she be excluded from any negotiations regarding the sale.

Her hand was shaking as she drafted a letter to her solicitor in London. She had not really considered what she would do with the hotel once she'd bought it, but at least it would not be lost entirely, and the good thing about the idea was that Lars would have his money returned. She pushed aside the thought that perhaps Brent's approval was the spur that drove her on.

She hardly slept that night. Her mind mulled over the problem of handling the Danton, and yet staying on in Norway near to Brent. She wanted to be near him, there was no doubt about that, and yet if he kept his word and left the hotel he would be lost to her for good.

In the morning, she was heavy eyed from lack of sleep and was late putting in an appearance for breakfast. As she entered the dining room, Eric was leaving, his collar turned up around his face, prepared for the chill of the mountain air.

"Kessie." He caught her arm. "I was just coming up to see you, I'll be back in little over a week, so you won't have time to get lonely."

"Where's Brent?" she asked and Eric's

face darkened. "It is always my brother you ask over, isn't it? Have you no feelings for me at all?"

Kessie rubbed her eyes tiredly. "Please Eric, don't quarrel with me now, I'm in no mood for it."

Eric put her aside and without another word went outside, and Kessie heard his voice ring out in the cold air. She hurried to the door and saw that Brent was already mounted, his horse pawing the ground, anxious to be away.

"Brent!" She called his name and he turned to look at her coldly.

"Yes, can I do anything for you?" he asked, and Kessie felt small and foolish under the grey disdain in his eyes.

For a moment she couldn't speak, then on a sudden impulse, she slipped her hand in her pocket and brought out the letter to the solicitor.

"Would you post that for me, please?" she asked. "I want it to arrive in London as soon as possible."

Without a word he leaned down from his

horse and took the letter. For a second his hand brushed hers and Kessie felt as though a fire was running through her veins.

She stepped back as Brent urged his horse forward and she watched as along with Eric he began to pick his way down the track towards the village below.

She longed to call him back, but she knew it would do no good. A warm glow began to light inside her when she thought about the letter she'd given him to post. If he read it, he would see that she was trying to put things right for Lars, paying him back the money he'd so foolishly spent on the hotel. But then, Brent wasn't the sort of man who read other people's letters.

Shivering, she returned to the hotel and closed the door behind her, wondering how long it would be before she saw Brent again. Eric had told her they would return in little over a week. Why then did she have this feeling that Brent had gone out of her life for good?

SEVEN

Lars moved ahead with his plans for the sauna spa almost immediately, no doubt secure, Kessie mused, in the knowledge that soon money would come in from the sale of the Danton.

The land behind the hotel was cleared of timber and local workers soon had the solid wooden cabins built to Lars' specifications. Kessie was surprised at the simplicity of the structures, but then the interiors were simple too, containing wooden benches and the braziers that held the hot stones.

"I think my customers will enjoy steaming off their aches and pains, and perhaps a little of their excess fat too!" Lars said with a smile, as Kessie and he sat in the office, going over the bookings.

Outside the window Kessie heard the clip clop of horses' hooves and her heart began to beat faster as she wondered if Brent had returned.

The door opened abruptly and the papers in Kessie's hand fell to the floor.

"I'm back and I think I can safely say the trip was successful." It was Eric's voice, not Brent's, and Kessie's disappointment was almost too much to bear.

Lars was on his feet, his arm around his son's shoulder, his face broken into a broad smile.

"That is good news, Eric. But where is Brent?" Lars asked. "Has he returned with you?"

"No," Eric shook his head. "I don't know where he's got to, but then Brent always did like his own way, as you well know, Father."

Lars' face darkened. "He has let me down once too often. I shall have sharp words to say to him when he does choose to come home."

"Perhaps he has found another way of

advertising the hotel," Kessie said quickly, attempting to pour oil on troubled waters, but Lars was adamant.

"He should have returned with his brother. It is inconsiderate of him to leave us wondering where he is. Good heavens, the boy could be lying somewhere injured for all we know!"

Kessie couldn't deny the sense in Lars' words. In this country, with storms a possibility at any time, it wasn't wise simply to go it alone with no one informed of your whereabouts.

"Well, we'll leave the subject for the moment. No doubt he'll think of calling us when it suits him," Lars said. "Come and see the progress we're making, son. I've had the men working day and night so that we can get things moving more quickly."

As Kessie watched them go, she felt a sudden urge to run after Eric and shake the truth out of him. There was more behind Brent's absence than was evident from Eric's silence. She felt sure that Brent would have given his brother some sort of message for Lars, but that Eric simply chose not to pass it on. She saw how he delighted in Lars' anger with Brent. Well, there was nothing she could accomplish by sitting brooding about it, she'd best get on with some work. There were still the bookings to go through for the following week.

As she ran her pen down the list of names, Kessie paused at that of Andrea Davidson and smiled. She was part of the hotel now, almost a fixture. The place wouldn't be the same if she decided to leave.

She heard a sudden noise through the window and looking out, Kessie saw a helicopter land neatly on the flat ground in front of the hotel. She pulled on a cardigan, anxious to see the new machine, and found that quite a few of the guests had come up with the same idea.

Lars was standing proudly by the side of the helicopter. He smiled and waved as he saw Kessie.

"Well, I've done it, I've mastered the infernal machine," he said, beaming. He slipped back into the cockpit and began explaining the controls to a few of the guests.

"So, you've convinced my father that he should buy a new toy," Eric was standing beside Kessie and she looked at him quickly.

"You know it's more than a toy, Eric," she said abruptly. "When the weather's bad the roads are impassable. Surely a helicopter is an investment."

Eric shook his head, a speculative look in his eyes, as he stared down at her.

"He's still a fine looking man, my father," he said softly. Sensing his implication, Kessie flushed.

"Don't be silly," she said, her voice rising. "I simply made a good suggestion that your father chose to take me up on." She sighed, shaking her head in exasperation. "Why do you always make things sound so drama-tic?"

"And why are you getting so flushed and angry if there is no truth in my words?" He caught her arm. "Are you setting your cap at my father now that you've found Brent is a dead loss?"

He smiled and pulled her closer to him.

"You'd be better off with me, I'm young and strong and I'll inherit all this one day." He waved his hand round the grounds, indicating the hotel and the foundations of the resort behind it.

"Oh?" Kessie tried to draw away. "You are very certain of yourself. What about Brent's share of everything?"

"I doubt if Brent's share would cover a postage stamp!" Eric laughed unpleasantly. "You see, you would be much better off settling for me."

Kessie pulled her arm away and began to walk back towards the hotel. She was acutely conscious of Eric keeping close to her side but she wouldn't look at him. She was seething inside, knowing that she'd been right about Eric all along. He would stop at nothing to diminish Brent in his father's eyes.

"Kessie, Eric, come along and sit with me. I'm bored and I need company!" Andrea waved to them from the lounge. Her dark curls were tied back with a large bandanna of pink and her softly flowing skirt was the same vivid colour.

"Why don't you practise your compliments on Andrea?" Kessie said a little sharply, and Eric gave her an amused glance.

"Oh, no, I've set my mind on conquering you, Kessie. Ever since that moment I saw you in my brother's arms I've wanted you."

He put his arm around her waist as they went towards Andrea, and short of causing a scene there wasn't much she could do about it.

"You two look very lovey dovey," Andrea said, her eyes wide. "I hope I'm not interrupting anything."

"Of course not," Kessie said, and Eric drew her even closer to his side, bending his head and touching her hair briefly with his lips.

"Don't worry, Andrea," he said. "There will be plenty of time for Kessie and me to be together."

"Oh," Andrea's eyes were full of speculation, "does that mean you've made up your mind about which man of the family you're going to settle for?"

"Don't be silly," Kessie said quickly. "I'm not settling for any of them, they're all yours if you want them."

Andrea put her head on one side. "Well, thanks for the invitation, I might just take it up." She smiled, her full lips close to Eric's ear as she whispered something.

Eric laughed out loud, turning to Kessie. "Andrea thinks I've a good chance of thawing the ice maiden in you. She doesn't know you very well, does she?"

He released Kessie and thankfully she moved away from him. "I don't know what you're talking about," she said, and Eric frowned.

"But we all know you're no ice maiden, don't we?" he said, and Kessie felt the colour rise to her cheeks.

"Oh, a dark horse, are you, Kessie?" Andrea said, in a tone of amusement, and Kessie bit her lip for a moment to stop the angry retort that longed to be spoken.

"Take no notice of Eric," she said at last.

"He simply likes to cause me embarrassment, though I can't think why."

Eric leaned towards her. "I like to see the colour come into your cheeks, Kessie," he said softly. "It always reminds me of the very first time I saw you."

Kessie was saved the effort of replying by the entry of Lars, who waved his hand to them eagerly.

"I'm taking the pilot who delivered the helicopter back down into the valley," he said. "Would anyone like to come with me for the trip?"

Andrea was the first to answer. She smiled up at Lars and stood beside him, her long hair covering her shoulders.

"I'd love to come, Lars," she said softly, and Lars tucked her arm under his and belatedly noticed Kessie.

"Come along, you must see this too. After all, it was your idea, wasn't it?"

A few minutes later, they were seated in the helicopter and the pilot who'd brought the machine up from the valley sat next to Kessie, smiling his approval of the way

Lars expertly lifted the machine from the plateau.

"Your ordinary flying obviously has stood you in good stead, Mr. Tolkelarson," he said. "You seem part of the machine."

Kessie's stomach turned over as they skimmed the edge of the plateau and hovered over the valley far below. The colours of the trees and water seemed to blend together and Kessie leaned forward in order to see better.

"It really is a lovely view." Andrea was sitting very close to Lars. "But I must admit that I'm a little nervous, the ground looks so very far away".

"You are quite safe," Lars smiled at Andrea, "and you must see how much more efficient this is as a means of travel. It will save hours of careful driving along icy roads, and will ensure we're not cut off from civilisation in an emergency."

Lars brought the helicopter down to land near the edge of the lake and as he switched off, the silence seemed to engulf them.

"Well, Mr. Tolkelarson," the pilot said,

"your weeks of practice have certainly paid off and you now have a good idea of handling the machine. But remember, there's nothing that beats experience, so keep at it. Just because you've got your licence it doesn't mean you know it all."

"I'm aware of that." Lars shook hands with the man. "Thanks for everything. Are you all right for transport back into town?"

"Yes," the pilot nodded, "I'm being picked up in the village in half an hour so I'd better be going."

Kessie wandered away and stood looking down into the water of the lake. Its depth reflected the blue bowl of the sky and the uneven line of the trees. It was very beautiful and peaceful, and looking over her shoulder, she smiled as she saw Lars and Andrea taking a walk, hand in hand.

"Hello, are you awake or asleep?" Brent's voice cut into her thoughts. Kessie looked up in astonishment, not really believing he was there in front of her.

"What are you doing here?" she asked, and he looked puzzled.

"Wasn't I expected? I thought that the helicopter was here to meet me."

"No," Kessie shook her head. "No one knew you were coming. Why didn't you send a message?"

Brent's lips tightened for an instant. "I did," he said, "with Eric, I might have known he'd fail to pass it on."

Kessie couldn't stop herself from staring at Brent, drinking in his presence. He caught her glance.

"Why are you staring at me like that, Kessie?" he asked softly. "It's as though you'd never really seen me before."

"And why are you suddenly being so nice to me?" she retorted. "I never know what sort of treatment I'll receive from you."

He leaned close to her, his arm touching hers, and Kessie drew a quick breath. What was it about this man that gave him the power to rouse her emotions so rapidly and unexpectedly?

"I learnt a few things when I was in London," Brent said, and Kessie looked at him questioningly. He smiled with maddening deliberation and shook his head.

"I'm sure you don't want to hear about me, though. Tell, when did Father take delivery of the helicopter?"

Kessie's mind was in a whirl as she struggled to make sense of his question.

"Oh, it was delivered today, as a matter of a fact," she said. "It's pure luck we're down here in the valley at this moment, otherwise you'd have had a long climb on foot up the mountain."

Brent didn't really seem to be listening. He leaned forward and pressed his lips lightly against hers, and Kessie moved away from him, sharply determined he wasn't going to weave his magic over her again.

"You have a nerve!" she said. "One minute you're practically accusing me of cheating your father deliberately, and the next you're forcing your attentions on me."

He smiled. "You look very lovely when you're angry." He turned and looked across the valley. "Where's my father gone to, why are you alone here?"

Kessie sighed. "I give up trying to make

any sense out of what you say." She shook her head. "Lars has taken Andrea for a walk. Is that all right by you?"

Her sarcasm was lost on him as he quite deliberately took her in his arms and held her close.

"I just have to kiss you," he said, and his lips were warm against hers, drawing the vitality from her so that she was unable to resist him. Weakly, she leaned against him, wanting the kiss to go on and on, unaware that she was winding her arms around his neck. It was only when he drew away from her with a smile on his face that she realised what a complete idiot she had made of herself.

"I hate you!" she said pushing at him. "Why can't you just leave me alone?" She was trembling as she moved away from him and stood at the edge of the silky lake, looking into the clear water.

Out of the corner of her eyes, she saw him following her and she stood up straight, trying to gather together the last remnants of her pride.

"I think I've had as much as I can take," she said and he was suddenly serious, his eyes looking down into hers, compelling her to meet his gaze.

"I've something to say to you, Kessie," he began, but there was a sudden shout and Andrea and Lars came into sight. Andrea was waving excitedly at them.

"Oh, you've decided to return, have you?" Lars said coldly, and Brent looked at him in surprise.

"Of course I've returned," he said abruptly. "I fully intended to all along, didn't Eric give you my message?"

"I've had no message," Lars said, "no message at all. It was inconsiderate of you to stay away, especially at this time, you must have known I'd need your help." Lars frowned. "But then you always went your own way. I don't like you to put the blame on to Eric. Come along, we shall return to the hotel and say no more about it."

"I did send you a message," Brent repeated. "Eric should have given it to you. Why do you always have to give him the benefit of the doubt?"

Lars almost exploded. "I do not treat one son different from the other," he shouted. But Brent stood his ground quite undismayed.

"Of course you do," he said flatly. "It's always been Eric, though, hasn't it, and yet he's the one who does the least to help you with the business."

Lars climbed into the helicopter, his face flushed as he gestured for them all to get in.

"We will discuss this back at the hotel," he said, "and not make a public brawl of our affairs."

The machine swung into the air and Kessie, pressed closely against Brent, longed to cover his hand with her own, to let him know that she at least was on his side. But one glance at his set face was enough to deter her from any such action.

Suddenly Lars moaned and leaned forward a little against the controls.

"What's wrong?" Andrea almost screamed in fright. "Lars, are you all right?"

"Yes, of course I am," he answered with

difficulty, "just a small pain, nothing much. I'm quite able to land safely so please don't anyone panic."

Brent leaned over him. "Are you sure, father?" he said anxiously, and with lips compressed, Lars nodded, heading the helicopter for the plateau. Even as he touched down, he slumped forward in his seat. In concern, Kessie tried her best to hold him but he was a dead weight and his lips were blue. Kessie frowned in concern.

"Has he ever been like this before?" she asked in a subdued voice, and Brent shook his head.

"Not as far as I know. Why, do you think it could be his heart?"

"It could be," Kessie agreed. "I believe that altitude sometimes affects the heart. It could be just a passing illness. Let's hope so."

Brent was the first to move. He scrambled out of the machine and nodded his head to Andrea.

"Go and tell Eric I'll need his help," he said, "and then telephone for a doctor." He smiled at her kindly, "and try not to worry, he's as strong as an ox, he'll be all right."

Andrea, white-faced, hurried away and Kessie helped Brent to move Lars nearer to the door.

"I can't help feeling guilty," she said softly. "If I hadn't talked him into getting the helicopter in the first place this wouldn't have happened."

"That's nonsense," Brent said flatly. "It would have happened some time, it was inevitable, no one's to blame. I could blame myself for arguing with him, but it's not constructive thinking.

The two brothers took Lars into the hotel and up to his room and Kessie stood for a moment in indecision before turning the corridor to her own room. She would go and change her clothes, by which time Lars should be comfortably settled.

There were sudden tears in her eyes as she sat on the bed and thought about Lars' kindness to her. She hoped fervently that the doctor would find nothing seriously wrong with him.

Brent was standing in the doorway of his father's room when Kessie went downstairs a few minutes later.

"Is it all right if I see him?" she asked nodding towards where Lars was sitting up in bed.

"It's all right, but don't stay too long," Brent said, and his hand touched her arm.

"Look, Kessie, I don't want you blaming yourself for this. You look worse than Father does. You're as white as a sheet."

"How can I help but blame myself?" Kessie said in a low voice. "It was I who put the idea of a helicopter into his mind."

"Nevertheless it's not your fault," Brent said firmly. "My father is a grown man, he makes his own decisions. This one happened to be the wrong one, that's all."

Kessie stood for a moment looking up at Brent. He smiled at her, and with lips trembling she turned from him and went into the room.

"Kessie, my dear, come here and don't look so worried. Lars Tolkelarson is not easily got rid of, I can tell you!"

He looked much fitter now. The colour had returned to his face and he was smiling. At his side, Andrea sat staring up at him, drinking him in with her eyes as though to reassure herself that he was really recovered.

Kessie gave Lars a quick kiss on his cheek and he squeezed her hand.

"I'm fine, now, really I am, so don't look like that, my dear. Anyway, none of it was your fault, so cheer up."

"Oh, Lars," Kessie sat beside him. "Thank goodness you're better. You gave us all a fright, I can tell you."

"He certainly did," Andrea echoed. She smiled at Kessie, a little shame-faced. "I'm sorry I made such a fuss, I was no help at all, was I?"

Lars laughed. "Come along, you two ladies, I'm not going to put up with long faces from you so cheer up or I'll send you both packing."

"We should go away," Andrea said. "You are supposed to be resting." She got to her feet and Lars protested.

"You're not leaving me alone already, are

you? How heartless of you."

Andrea smiled. "Oh, you don't know how heartless I can be, but you'll find out now that I've got you at my mercy."

She smiled at Kessie. "Come on, you're going to back me up, aren't you? If we leave him on his own, he might just get some sleep."

Kessie nodded and followed Andrea to the door. She looked back and Lars beckoned to her, his face serious.

"Kessie," he said, "come here just a minute. I want you to do me a favour."

"Of course," Kessie said at once, and Lars smiled. "I want you to persuade Brent to stay on here a while, at least until I'm fitter," he said. "Will you do that for me?"

"Yes," Kessie said quickly. "I'll do my best to persuade him, but you mustn't worry yourself about the business. Think of yourself for a change."

Outside Brent was just coming towards his father's room. He looked at Andrea and Kessie questioningly.

"How is he now?" He stood beside Kessie,

so tall and with such a serious look on his face that she wanted to kiss him.

It was Andrea who answered. "He seems much improved, he's resting now. Anything I can do, please ask, I'll be only too happy to help. I've become so fond of your father, Brent..." her voice trailed away and Brent touched her arm lightly. "I know, and thank you for your concern."

Andrea returned his smile and hurried away, her long hair flowing behind her.

"She's in love with my father," he said, and Kessie nodded, wondering how he felt about such a situation. Would he resent Andrea?

He must have read her thoughts, because he turned to her so suddenly that she had no time to avoid his eyes.

"I don't mind at all if they hit it off," he said smoothly, as though answering a question. "On the contrary, I think Andrea will be good for Father. She's bossy enough in the nicest possible way to see that he looks after himself a little better."

Kessie began to walk down the corridor

and Brent kept pace with her. She struggled to find the right words to ask him to stay and she was finding it difficult, because although the request was made by Lars, she knew it was echoed in her own heart.

"Lars is hoping you'll stay on for a while now," she said at last. "He does need you here, Brent, and he recognises that fact."

"And you, Kessie," Brent asked, "do you want me to stay on here, as well?"

She was on her guard at once. He had thought her a fortune hunter once, she was not going to give him the opportunity again.

"It's a matter of complete indifference to me," she said, "except that I feel Lars needs you now, perhaps more than ever."

"I see." Brent's voice carried a hint of amusement, and it brought the colour flaming to Kessie's cheeks. Why did he always have to laugh at her?

"Once Lars is better," she said on an impulse, "I'll be leaving here, so you needn't worry that I'm going to cast my net in your direction."

"Oh, where are you going?" Brent asked in

the way of someone making a polite enquiry, though not very much interested in
the answer.

"I'm returning to London," Kessie said.
"I'm going to buy the Danton back from
your father and try to make a go of it."

Brent was silent for a moment and Kessie
almost willed him to speak. To say, or even
hint, that he would like her to stay on, but
he said nothing.

"Well?" she challenged him, "don't you
think it's a good idea?"

"Maybe," he said, "but good ideas often
don't work out in practice."

"Thank you for your vote of confidence,"
she said hotly. "You are enough to make
anyone swear!"

"Are you losing your temper again?" he
asked smoothly. "You are more tempera-
mental than our lady film star."

"Oh, you're so supercilious and superior,
aren't you?" she said. "Have you no feelings,
are you just a machine?"

He pulled her in his arms and pressed her
close, his hand holding her head tightly so

180

that she couldn't move. His mouth sought hers and the kiss was sweet and passionate and Kessie's blood sang in her veins.

"Let me go!" She made an effort to push him away but she was weak against his strength. Her senses were deserting her and all she could do was to hold on to him while longing for him surged through her. Why couldn't he be kissing her like this because he loved her, not just because he thought it was amusing to see her losing control?

"Let me go!" She slapped out at his face hard and her fingers left red marks along the lean brownness of his cheek. He grasped her even harder, pressing her against the wall of the corridor, his hand forcing her face upward so that she could not avoid his searching lips. She gave herself up to him then, knowing that it was useless to try fighting herself as well as him. He kissed her long and hard and she felt her senses swamping her body so that her mind no longer seemed to function. If he had picked her up at the moment and carried her into one of the rooms, she felt she would have been powerless to resist. She was like putty in his hands, and the knowledge frightened her.

He released her at last, though his body was still close to hers, and she knew she didn't want him to stop kissing her. She felt flushed almost as though she had a fever, and she wanted to fling herself to her knees, to beg him to love her as she loved him.

"I hate you?" she said in a whisper and he laughed, his teeth flashing white, his grey eyes unreadable.

"Do you?" he said, "or is it that you love me and won't confess it?"

"How can you be so conceited?" she said, staring up at him, still feeling the magic of his lips on hers, still bemused with the intensity of the emotions he had aroused in her.

"It's not conceit," he said, "it's simply recognising the truth, something you apparently are incapable of."

"Oh, leave me alone." She put her hands to her face. "I can't even think straight any more."

"Very well," he said, "I'll leave you alone,

182

but that won't stop you from wanting me, will it?" He moved a pace away from her and it took all her powers of control not to fling herself back into his arms.

His eyes were mocking now and she became aware that her hair was hanging in untidy tangles around her shoulders, having fallen from the ribbon that had held it. Her face must surely be flushed and her throat ached with unshed tears.

"I'm going to my room," she said with as much dignity as she could muster and she pushed back her hair, shaking it out of her eyes, trying her best not to let the tears of mortification spill over.

"My room," he reminded her softly. "I'll think of you lying in my bed, and remember that first night when you slept in my arms all night."

"You're so cruel!" she said in a choked voice. "The sooner I leave here, the better."

She almost ran from him, and in spite of her brave words, she knew that when she left Norway she would leave her heart behind.

EIGHT

Lars seemed to make a complete recovery, and in a very short time he was up and on his feet, dealing with matters concerning the new project of the saunas as though he had never been ill.

Kessie smiled as she saw him in the corridor and he put his arms around her shoulders.

"I want you to come to the office in about an hours' time," he said. "I'd like a meeting with Brent and Eric present so that we can sort out a few little problems that have cropped up."

"I don't know if you should even be out of bed," Kessie said. "Why can't you leave things to Brent now that you've persuaded him to stay for the time being?"

"Well, he has been good to me," Lars conceded. "I don't know what I'd have done without him over these past weeks."

It gave Kessie a warm glow of pleasure to hear Lars praise Brent, and he must have sensed something of what she was feeling.

"You still feel that you are in love with Brent, don't you?" he asked, and the colour flew to her cheeks as Lars touched her shoulder.

"You don't need to speak, I can see the answer in your face, but I still wish you preferred Eric."

"I must go," Kessie said quickly, "but I'll be at the office in precisely an hour's time."

She hurried away before Lars could make any more comments about her feelings. She felt confused and unhappy enough as it was, without having to try to explain things to Lars.

"Kessie!" Andrea was waving to her excitedly and Kessie sighed, knowing she couldn't avoid her without appearing rude.

"Come and talk to me," Andrea said in her

usual imperious way, catching Kessie's arm and indicating that she sit down beside her. "I just have to tell someone my news!" she said. "Lars has told me to keep it to myself but I'll burst if I don't talk about it to someone, and I know you'll be discreet."

"What is it?" Kessie asked, knowing already what Andrea was going to say.

"Lars and I are getting engaged." Andrea's eyes gleamed with excitement. "Oh, Kessie, I'm so happy, I don't know how to stop myself from shouting it from the roof tops."

"I'm sure you'll both be very happy," Kessie said in genuine pleasure. "Will you miss your career?"

Andrea laughed. "You know as well as I do how far that had gone, soap ads and at best a small walking-on part. Oh no, I won't miss any of that."

She looked around her. "It's so lovely here, I feel more at home than ever before in my life. You could say this is the only real home I've ever had." She sighed. "And what's so wonderful is that Lars and I are so much in love! Only don't tell him I've confided in you!"

Kessie smiled. "I'll pretend I haven't heard a word you've said."

"Now," Andrea leaned forward, "what about you Kessie. Which one of these boys are you going to marry?"

"Neither of them!" Kessie spoke firmly. "In fact I shall probably be returning to London shortly."

Andrea's face fell. "Oh, no!" She shook back her long dark hair. "What shall I do without you? I'll have no one to talk to."

Kessie couldn't help laughing. "You'll find someone, I've no doubt about that. Anyway, I won't be going just yet, and please, Andrea, don't mention it to anyone."

Andrea giggled. "It is a day for little secrets, isn't it? But, I'm glad you confided in me."

It amazed Kessie how glibly the words had slipped out as she told Andrea she might be leaving Norway. The idea had slowly been forming in the back of her mind since she'd written to her solicitors in London, but she hadn't put it into words, not even to herself.

"You're far away," Andrea's voice broke into her reverie, "a penny for your thoughts."

Kessie smiled. "They're not worth it. I'd better go, Andrea, I'm a working girl, don't forget, not a lady of leisure like you."

Kessie hurried to her room and her heart began to beat faster as she saw the letter propped up on her dressing table. One glance told her it was from London. Perhaps by now the negotiations were complete and she'd be the owner of the Danton again.

Her fingers shook as she tore open the envelope and read the letter inside. At first she couldn't believe what was written there. In cold impersonal tones she was informed that the Danton had been sold to a higher bidder. She sank down on to the bed, the letter slipping from her fingers. She simply couldn't believe that the Danton was gone out of her grasp for ever. Even when Lars bought it, it seemed as though it was still in the family somehow, and now it had gone to strangers.

She was startled by a sudden knocking on

the door and quickly she tried to compose herself.

"Are you all right?" Brent stood in the doorway, his eyes shrewd as they looked first at her and then at the letter on the floor. "Not bad news, I hope."

He crossed the room in long easy strides and retrieved the letter before Kessie could stop him.

"Is this why you look so desolate?" His tone was kind. "Because your family business has been sold?"

She nodded, trying hard to speak normally, but there was a lump in her throat and her distress must have been obvious.

"It's quite a blow to find it's no longer within my reach," she said at last, and Brent sat down on the bed beside her. Gently he took her hand in his and the touch was one of kindness, so different from his casual embraces that Kessie looked up at him, her eyes full of tears.

"I know it's silly of me," she said, "but I feel as though I've lost something precious."

"I can understand that," Brent said, "but

Kessie, it's people that make a place a home, not bricks and mortar."

"I know that." Kessie spoke with feeling. How would she cope when she had no contact with Brent, when he left his father's hotel as he surely would one day?

"Look, we have to go down to the office," Brent said slowly. "Can you manage it or shall I make excuses for you?"

"I'm all right," Kessie said with more confidence than she was feeling.

"Good girl." Brent smiled down at her and strangely she felt very close to him at that moment, closer even than the times when he took her in his arms and kissed her passionately. Then she always felt that he was laughing at her, but his attitude now was one of kindness and consideration and Kessie was grateful for it.

"Ah, there you both are, I was beginning to wonder if you had got lost on the way!"

Lars sat behind his desk and Eric stood at the window, staring out as though he had no real interest in the proceedings.

"Well," Lars leaned forward, "I have made

up my mind that you, Kessie and Eric here will handle the new saunas between you."

He smiled, "Eric can handle the sports equipment and organise the programme for our guests to keep fit by, and you, dear Kessie, can do much the same as you're doing here, see to the bookings and that sort of thing." He leaned back in his chair. "Brent, you can stay to help me here in the hotel, at least for a little while until I'm fit again."

Kessie felt her spirits drop. "Don't you think it might be better if the health spa was handled by Brent and Eric and I stayed on here?" she suggested. She couldn't see herself working alongside Eric very successfully.

"No," Lars shook his head. "I want Brent to ease himself slowly into my position here, so that I can become semi-retired and enjoy life a little."

"I shan't be staying on here any longer than is necessary," Brent said mildly. "You know that, don't you, Father?"

"I know, my boy," Lars said with a smile,

"and in the circumstances I don't blame you. But remember, every little bit of training you receive here will stand you in good stead for the future. Isn't that right?"

A look passed between father and son and Kessie had the distinct impression that there was some secret between them.

"That's right," Brent agreed, "and of course I'll do my best to get everything moving while I am here. You still have to take things easy you know."

"Don't remind me!" Lars said good naturedly and smiled warmly at Andrea. "I'm constantly being told that by someone who has become very special to me." He drew Andrea forward and she clung to his arm, smiling up at him with open adoration.

"Now for my own special news," he said. "Nothing to do with business, but as you're all here I'd like to make an announcement."

"I don't think what you're going to say is going to come as any surprise to us," Brent said dryly, and Lars laughed.

"Maybe not, but I intend to make a big production of it all the same. Andrea and I are engaged as from this minute."

He took out a box of lush velvet, and nestling inside it was a large glittering diamond ring. He slipped it on to Andrea's finger and then bent down ceremoniously and kissed her.

"Congratulations!" Kessie said warmly, feeling the tears burn her eyes. "I know you'll both be very happy."

Andrea, with her usual flair for the dramatic, kissed Kessie on both cheeks and then went to the brothers in turn.

"I'm so happy!" she said. "I want everyone to be happy with me."

"Well, go on," Lars said, smiling indulgently. "I'll give Kessie official time off so that she can sit with you and discuss things that you women talk of at a time like this. Will that suit you?"

"Oh, Lars, you're so understanding!" Andrea said, kissing him soundly. "I couldn't bear to be left on my own just now."

Kessie could sympathise. She suddenly felt very homesick and strangely lonely, in spite of the fact that Andrea was walking along the corridor at her side, chattering her head off.

Kessie couldn't understand the emotions that were sweeping over her. She supposed it must be a combination of events, the sale of the Danton and the fact of seeing Lars and Andrea so happy and so obviously in love.

"You're looking sad," Andrea said. "Don't worry, Kessie, you'll find the man you're looking for some day, just as I did. It was quite out of the blue for me. I never thought when I booked in here that I'd meet the man I would eventually marry."

"Oh, I'm just wondering what the future holds for me," Kessie said. "You know I was thinking of returning to London to work, but I don't know what I'd do there even if I did go back." The Danton was the only home she'd known. It would be too painful to pass it and to see it in other hands, perhaps even torn down to make way for some new monstrosity that would have central heating but no character.

On the other hand, the thought of working

alongside Eric wasn't one that appealed to her.

"Oh, you mustn't go back to London!" Andrea said in dismay. "I can't picture the place without you, you seem to be part of the Sornefjord."

Kessie laughed. "That's exactly what I was thinking about you a little while ago."

"Really?" Andrea was pleased. "Yes, I suppose I was one of the first guests to arrive here."

"You gave me my first problem as manageress," Kessie confessed, and Andrea's brows were raised like silky black arches.

"Oh, tell me about it!" Andrea said. "In what way was I a problem?"

"Remember the delay about giving you the keys to your room?" Kessie said, and Andrea nodded.

"Oh yes, you looked so cool and capable I was terrified of you," Andrea said. "You organised me into having a cup of coffee and waiting in the lounge and all along I was wondering if I should play the part of the star and have a tantrum or something."

"I'm very glad you didn't!" Kessie feelingly. "Things were bad enough anyway, you were double booked and the other guest was already settled in the suite you should have had."

"Good heavens!" Andrea's eyes were wide. "How did you manage? I mean the rooms I have now are so comfortable."

"They were mine," Kessie said smiling. "I ended up in Brent's room and have been there ever since."

Andrea's eyes were astute. "And not unhappy to be there, dare I say?"

Kessie knew her colour was rising. "What makes you say that?"

"Intuition," Andrea said. "But if it's a tender subject, I'll say no more about it."

Kessie rose to her feet. "I think I'll stretch my legs a little," she said, changing the subject. "Do you feel like coming for a walk?"

Andrea nodded. "All right, I suppose a little fresh air won't kill me. I'll just get a jacket. Although the sun is shining I still find this place cold, don't you?"

She hurried up the stairs and Kessie stared out of the window, wondering if her feelings for Brent were transparent to everyone. He was even beginning to tease her himself now, telling her she must be in love with him.

She envied Andrea for the simplicity of her life. She'd wanted Lars and she'd got him. Why couldn't she, Kessie, find things as straightforward?

"Here I am, I didn't keep you long, did I?" Andrea was wearing a soft fur jacket in pure white and it set off her dark hair to perfection. She was enough to turn any man's head. Beside her, Kessie felt very brown and ordinary.

"Come along, then, fresh air fiend!" Andrea said, laughing. "I hope you realise I wouldn't brave the cold for just anyone."

It was cold, in spite of the sun slanting in the sky. A cool wind was blowing and high on the mountain crevices white snow lay like glazed sugar.

Kessie took a deep breath and the air was like wine. Why was it, then, that she sometimes longed so much for the dust and dirt of London?

Andrea must have been reading her thoughts, because when she spoke it was on the same subject.

"I'd never want to return to London and the bright lights," she said. "Not now. I've had my fill of all that."

"It's certainly lovely here," Kessie said. "The view into the valley is breathtaking."

Andrea laughed. "I'd prefer it from the warmth and comfort of the hotel, quite frankly. I'm not one for being in the great outdoors."

She put a hand on Kessie's arm. "Look, if you want to talk to me, I'm quite a sympathetic listener, in spite of prattling on most of the time."

"Thanks," Kessie said. But how could she bring herself to tell anyone that she was hopelessly in love with a man who didn't really know she existed?

As if conjured up by her thoughts, Brent came into view, striding out on long legs towards them.

"Hello there!" Andrea waved in her un-inhibited way and Kessie watched as Brent drew nearer, his hair gleaming in the sun.

She stood back a little as Andrea took Brent's arm and hugged it to her.

"You haven't said what you think of your new step mother-to-be," she said playfully, and Brent glanced down at her, a smile on his face.

"I happen to think she's very beautiful," he said, and Kessie couldn't help the absurd dart of jealousy that caught her breath.

"I think I'll turn back now," she said, and Brent merely nodded. Andrea gave her a quick glance but said nothing.

As Kessie trudged back up the slope alone, she felt anger grow inside her. Brent was always doing the unexpected. She had been sure he would leave Andrea and return to the hotel at the same time as she herself did.

She glanced back over her shoulder but they were already out of sight. She sighed. She would never learn to understand Brent if she lived to be a hundred!

Suddenly, her foot caught in a fallen

branch and tipped her off balance. As she fell there was a sudden sharp pain in her ankle and she gave a little cry pulling at the branch, trying to free her foot. But the branch would not move and Kessie realised that she was stuck fast. She tried breaking off the smaller of the branches to use as a lever but all she succeeded in doing was scratching her hand on the roughness of the tree bark.

"What's happened to you, then?" Brent was standing looking down at her, amusement written plain on his face.

"I should think that's obvious even to you!" Kessie ground the words out, hating him and yet trembling as he bent down and caught hold of her ankle, lifting it free of the branch with infuriating ease.

"You are not safe to trust out on your own!" he said. "Aren't you lucky I chose to come back now? Otherwise you might have been sitting her for several hours."

"I'd have freed myself somehow." Kessie got to her feet, wincing a little at the pain in her ankle.

"What's wrong, are you hurt?" Brent leaned forward. "Your ankle is a little swollen but I don't think anything is broken. Come on, lean on me."

There was no point in refusing his help. He put his arm around her waist and she felt the blood surge hotly in her veins.

"Put your arm around me," he instructed. "Come along, I won't bite you."

Slowly, they made their way back up the rugged face of the hill.

"You'd better rest when we get back to the hotel," Brent said. "Keep your foot up for an hour or two until the swelling goes down."

Kessie didn't answer him. There seemed nothing to say. Once again he'd made her feel foolish and incompetent. More than that, she longed for him to kiss her, to take her in his arms under any terms She was a fool, she knew it, but she couldn't fight any longer the feeling Brent aroused in her.

"You're very quiet," he observed, stopping for a moment so that she was forced to stop too.

"There's nothing to talk about," she replied, and he gave a short laugh.

"On the contrary, there is a great deal to talk about, but this is neither the time nor the place."

"What do you mean?" Kessie asked, afraid to look up at him in case he read the longing in her eyes.

"I'll tell you when the time comes," he said with tantalising casualness.

She shivered and Brent tipped her face up. "Are you cold?" he asked. "Or are you affected by me holding you this way?"

She bit her lips for a moment, biting back the sharp reply that longed to be spoken. He was baiting her and she was not going to rise to it.

"Why should I be affected to you one way or the other?" she said, as coldly as she could, and Brent laughed, turning her to face him and placing his hands on her waist.

"Could it be that you are in love with me?" Brent asked, and Kessie pushed him away.

"You are so infuriatingly sure of yourself, aren't you?" she said. "Well, I'm one girl who isn't going to fall under your spell. I don't care a jot about you!"

She made off towards the hotel without waiting for him to help her. It was painful, limping along, trying to reach the hotel as quickly as possible, but her pride would not let her stop and accept his help.

"What's wrong, Kessie?" Eric came out of the entrance just as she arrived there, and she made a wry face.

"Oh, nothing, really, I twisted my ankle, that's all. Do you think you could help me to my room, Eric?"

As soon as the words were spoken she regretted them, but Brent was behind her now and she leaned on Eric's arm a little more heavily than was strictly necessary.

Eric took her by surprise by sweeping her up into his arms and carrying her towards the lift. Kessie caught sight of Brent's face and far from being annoyed as she hoped he would be he was looking distinctly amused.

In her room, Eric set her down on the bed "Kessie," he said, "do I take this as a sign that you want to be more than friendly?" He put his arm around her shoulders. "I've been so tired of you giving me the brush off but I knew you didn't really mean it."

He pressed her back on the bed and kissed her lips passionately. He was breathing heavily and Kessie suddenly felt frightened.

"Eric, if you really care about me, you'll treat me with respect," she murmured. "This isn't the way I want things to happen at all."

He moved away from her. "All right Kessie, if you want me to be all formal and correct then I shall be. You'll see I can be just as much of a charmer as my brother if I set my mind to it."

He went out and closed the door and Kessie sighed with relief. She'd got rid of him for the present but he wasn't one to give in so easily. He had something up his sleeve and she had the feeling she wouldn't like it when she finally found out what his plans were.

She lay back on the bed and closed her eyes. Her ankle hurt and all she wanted to do at this moment was to sleep and forget all about the Tolkelarson family. But sleep just wouldn't come, and sighing she resigned herself to staring dry-eyed at the ceiling.

The opening of the sauna spa was quite a success. Fortunately, the weather was quite good and the roads passable and several reporters came to cover the event.

Andrea seemed to be having a fine time, Kessie thought with humour. When any light flashed, Andrea could be depended upon to be posing for the picture, her slim body covered by a towel, her long hair flowing down her back.

In reality, the heat of the saunas was too much for her and she rubbed a shiny nose, grimacing at Kessie with wry resignation

"If I stay in the steam any longer, I'll fade away into nothing!" she said. "How can people do that to themselves?"

Kessie shrugged. "I suppose the idea of keeping fit appeals to people, especially when on holiday. It seems more like fun then."

"Well, it's certainly not my idea of fun." Andrea looked at her closely. "Why are you looking so down in the mouth? You should be enjoying yourself today."

"Why?" Kessie asked. "All this was Lars' idea, not mine, I'm just an onlooker."

"Don't be so modest, Kessie," Andrea reproved her, "You know that you gave Lars every assistance. It's as much thanks to you that this scheme got off the ground as to anybody."

"I suppose so," Kessie said, but even to herself, her voice lacked conviction.

Lars joined them, beaming. "Well, it seems as though my little idea has gone down well with the public," he said. "All the sauna cabins are already in use and the restaurant is bulging at the seams."

Andrea smiled up at him. "It's all beautiful, Lars, I was just saying as much to Kessie."

Lars grinned hugely. "Yes, and perhaps I wouldn't have managed such excellent equipment without the sale of the Danton."

Kessie felt a pang. It still hurt to think of the family hotel being sold, though obviously Lars didn't realise how she felt. He would never intentionally be unkind.

"Well, I'd better get on, " Lars said. "But put on your prettiest gowns for the party tonight, won't you, girls? You too, Kessie."

She nodded, making a vague reply, though the way she felt at the moment it was doubtful that she would ever turn up at the party.

She edged her way out of the steam of the cabin, it was over-hot even in the entrance. If she rested a while, she might feel more like celebrating.

As she reached the staircase, she saw Brent standing there, talking to one of the guests. His tall, lean frame had its usual effect on Kessie and she cursed herself for being a fool, even as the hot colour came to her cheeks. He turned, and seeing her, came over.

"Why aren't you over at the cabins, getting your share of the congratulations?" he said, and for the first time Kessie wondered if Brent was peeved because she and Eric had been put in to manage the resort and not him.

"I'm tired," she said flatly, and moved past

him, walking slowly up the stairs. Her ankle was still painful though she tried her best not to let it show.

"You look a little pale, come to think of it." Brent fell into step beside her. "Doing too much, I dare say, trying to prove to Father what an eager little beaver you are."

She gave him a withering look, "And what's that supposed to mean?"

"What do you think it's supposed to mean?" he countered and Kessie shook her head.

"It sounds as though you think I'm trying to ingratiate myself with your father."

"Aren't you?" Brent smiled down at her with the usual touch of amusement he seemed to reserve for her.

"No, I'm not, why should I?" Kessie asked flatly. "What could I possibly gain from it?"

"A secure job?" Brent caught her arm. "Look, Kessie, why are you always on the defensive with me?"

"I'm not!" She tried to draw away but he wouldn't release her.

"Come here." He drew her gently against

him, holding her head against his shoulder so that she couldn't struggle. Tiredly, she relaxed in his arms, wanting him to continue to hold her in such a comforting way.

"You are a silly little girl at times, Kessie." His voice was gentle. "Such a prickly little thing." He smoothed back her hair and she closed her eyes, not thinking, just allowing herself to be carried away by Brent's unexpected solicitude.

"You need a rest," he said. "I shall tell Father so, it's time you had a holiday."

She moved then out of the circle of his arms. "I don't want a holiday," she said, and it was the truth. Where would she go and what would she do without Brent near her?

Slowly, she stepped back a pace, and avoiding Brent's eyes made for the door of her room.

He followed her and she didn't resist as he entered the room behind her.

She sat down on the bed a little shakily, and Brent stood looking down at her, a smile on his lips.

"I know what's wrong with you, Kessie,"

he said. "You're in love with me, aren't you? I've tried to tell you so before but you're too stubborn to listen."

"I'm not in love with you," she said flatly, but the lie sounded unconvincing even to herself.

Brent shrugged, "You'll have to admit it one day, why not now?"

"Oh, leave me alone," she said. "What do you know about my feelings?"

"A lot more than you give me credit for." He turned and walked to the door.

"I'd have a sleep if I were you, there are circles under your eyes as large as saucers."

"Thanks for making me feel so unattractive!" Kessie said with sarcasm. "That's all I need."

"You're beautiful," Brent said simply. "I've always thought so ever since that first night we spent together in the hut."

Kessie was disarmed by the change of tone. She stared up at him, unable to think of anything to say.

He smiled. "Your eyes grow so large when you're angry or bewildered, you have such an expressive face that you give all your thoughts away."

She turned away from him, feeling vulnerable and exposed. Brent laughed.

"All right, I'll leave you in peace. Have a good rest so that you'll be able to enjoy Father's celebration tonight. Don't forget that I claim the first dance."

He went out then and it was to Kessie as though the sun had gone in. She shivered and tears came to her eyes. She loved Brent so very much and all he felt for her was a sort of amused indulgence.

After she'd showered, she lay on the bed and closed her eyes. She was so very tired, she couldn't even make the effort to put out the clothes she was going to wear that night. Her mind became woolly and her last thought was of Brent holding out his arms to her, inviting her to dance.

She was woken by a rapping on the door and she sat up startled, brushing the tangled hair away from her face.

"Who is it?" she called and the door opened to admit Eric. He smiled when he saw her and placed a box with a single orchid on the table next to the bed.

"Don't be long," he said. "The party will start without you otherwise."

"Oh, thank you Eric, I'll get ready straight away." She felt uneasy as always when he was present and she scrambled off the bed, straightening her clothes.

To her surprise, he merely gave her a quick, almost formal bow and retreated from the room. She stared after him, wondering once more what he could be planning. She didn't trust him but she couldn't really see how he could do anything to upset her tonight. After all there would be crowds of people round the place.

She dressed quickly and after a moment's hesitation, pinned on the orchid. It seemed churlish not to accept it, perhaps it was a sort of peace offering on Eric's part. He certainly seemed to have changed in the last few days.

As she descended the stairs, she saw with a stirring of uneasiness that Eric was waiting for her. He stood there smiling, watching her come down the stairs with the soft blue skirt of her dress billowing behind her.

"You look very beautiful," he said, and she made an effort to return his smile, though in her heart she wished it could have been Brent saying those things to her.

The room was already crowded when they entered together and the first person she saw was Brent. He frowned as he met her gaze and she looked away knowing the he was already condemning her for being with Eric.

As she settled herself beside him, Kessie was aware of Brent's scrutiny. On her other side, Eric put a proprietary arm round the back of her chair.

"That's a pretty dress," Brent said, "and an orchid, no less, to go with it. Your admirer knew what you were going to wear obviously."

It seemed too complicated to explain that she had chosen the dress after Eric had presented her with the orchid, so Kessie said nothing.

"Who is this unknown admirer?" Brent

persisted, and Eric leaned forward.

"I gave the flower to Kessie if you must know. Sorry you didn't think of it yourself, are you?"

"I am as a matter of fact," Brent said, "but I would have chosen a tawny colour, something to bring out the flame that I know is there beneath the surface."

His reply seemed to anger Eric. "What are you insinuating?" he said quickly. "Come on, let's have it straight."

"I'm not insinuating anything," Brent said mildly. "I'm telling you there is more to Kessie than meets the eye, that's all."

"Will you stop talking about me as though I wasn't here?" Kessie said. "And please stop arguing, you'll spoil your father's evening if you keep this up. See, he's glowering at the pair of you right now."

Lars rose to his feet and the room suddenly became silent. All eyes turned to him and he was a commanding figure with his huge frame and the thick crisp hair that stood away from his leonine head.

"I would like to make an announcement,"

214

he said. "My son Eric has made me very proud and happy by telling me he is to marry the daughter of a life-long friend of mind. Will you all make a toast to Eric and Kessie."

Numb with amazement, Kessie felt herself being drawn to her feet and then there was a sea of smiling faces around her, except for Brent who had become very cold and withdrawn. Eric pulled her close to him and then he was slipping a ring on to her nerveless finger and everyone was clapping.

"Come along, Kessie," Eric said, smiling almost in triumph. "Aren't you going to kiss your fiancé?"

NINE

Afterwards, Kessie had little memory of how she'd got through the rest of that terrible evening. Perhaps the worst part had been sitting next to a morose and silent Brent who had not even looked her way once the announcement of the engagement had been made.

Once in the privacy of her own room, she tore the orchid from her dress, crushing it between her fingers as if by doing that small act of revenge she could wipe out Eric's appalling behaviour. There was no way she could ever bring herself to marry him, and she knew she would have to tell him so in no uncertain terms, and yet she still wore his ring on her finger.

He had very cleverly forced her into silence when she felt like denouncing him to the whole assembled party of people.

"Don't break my father's heart," he'd whispered in her ear, "let him enjoy the prospect of our marriage if only for a short time. Remember his heart isn't as strong as it might be."

So she had remained silent, and even now, a few days after the event, she wasn't sure how she should handle it.

With a sigh, she left her room and went downstairs. There was still work to be done for the bookings in the new health resort had come in thick and fast. She held her head high and managed to smile a little at guests who were happily unaware of the turmoil within her.

She was about to leave the hotel and make her way across the grounds towards the new building when she saw Brent coming towards her. Her heart began to beat so rapidly that she could scarcely breathe. She hadn't caught even a glimpse of him since the night of the party.

"Brent," she said holding our her hand to touch his arm tentatively, "may I speak with you for a moment, I won't keep you long."

His eyes were cold as he looked down at her, but he inclined his head in assent and led her towards the office.

"Yes, what is it?" he said, closing the door, shutting them in the smallness of the room together.

"It's about the other night. I just wanted to explain, to tell you how I felt about it."

"I can see how you feel about it." He looked down at the diamond ring glinting on her finger. "I don't really see there is any need for words, do you?"

"But Brent," she protested, "I knew nothing about it. I was absolutely shocked when Eric made the announcement."

"You really expect me to believe that?" he said, his eyebrows raised, a sardonic smile on his face. "You were wearing the orchid he'd given you and to me that's not an act of indifference."

"Please, Brent." Kessie searched in her mind for the right words but they just wouldn't come. "You've got to believe me, I want no part of this engagement. I'm only wearing the ring for the sake of not upsetting your father."

"Oh, really, Kessie." Brent seemed to lose patience. "Why not stop all this pretence. You wanted to marry into the family and now it seems you have your wish so make the most of it. You won't get any other offers."

His tone was insulting and Kessie got to her feet, the colour hot in her cheeks.

"If you mean from you then don't worry. I wouldn't marry you if you were the last man on earth!"

"Well, now we both know where we stand perhaps we can end this rather futile conversation."

He opened the door for her and on a surge of anger she stood before him, trembling so much she could hardly speak.

"I hate you, Brent Tolkelarson!" she said in a low voice. "It was the worse thing that ever happened to me when I met you, I wish I'd never set eyes on you."

He didn't even bother to reply, he simply stood looking down at her, waiting in silence for her to leave the room.

She swept past him and out into the corridor and almost walked into Eric's arms.

"Kessie." He caught her when she stumbled against him, and knowing that Brent was looking on, Kessie allowed herself to lean against Eric.

"Kessie, are you all right?" Eric said, his eyes going from her flushed face to Brent's smile of amusement.

"Yes, of course I am, Eric," she said, "but I could use a cup of tea. Would you like to come with me?"

"Of course." He took her arm and Kessie walked along beside him, her anger cooling and anxiety taking its place. She should not allow Eric to think she was encouraging him in any way at all, and yet here she was arm in arm with him.

She sat at the table watching him as he set about pouring the tea for her. From the look on his face he was only too happy about the unexpected warmth of her response.

"Look, Kessie," he said, at last. "I know things haven't gone exactly evenly between us at times, but don't you think we might make a go of it, if we got together? After all, my father feels we could run the resort successfully between us and if we were married, it would be an ideal arrangement."

Kessie's eyes widened. "But Eric, you know I'm not in love with you." She glanced away from him. "I don't mean to be unkind, Eric, but I might as well tell you the truth. I'm in love with Brent and there's nothing I can do about it."

He stared at her, a look of determination on his face. "I'm not taking no for an answer, Kessie," Eric said. "You are just mixed up at this moment. Given time you'll get over your infatuation and then you'll realise he's just a man like any other."

She shrugged. "Maybe you're right, but I can't say I'll marry you, Eric. It just wouldn't be fair to anyone."

He put his hand out to cover hers. "Look Kessie, I'm willing to take that chance if you are. Come on, what have you got to lose?"

"Oh, leave me alone now, please, Eric." Kessie rubbed her eyes. "I just can't begin to think straight right now. Let me have some time to consider what you've said, will you?"

"All right," he smiled. "We'll forget about it for now but don't keep me waiting too long. I'm getting impatient."

He smiled as though to soften his words. "Well, I'd better be getting back to work now," he said after a pause. "There's a lot to get through today. Oh, and by the way I'm supposed to let you know that Father wants to see us all in the office later on." He leaned over and gave her a quick kiss on her cheek and Kessie felt so defeated and unhappy at the way events seemed to be sweeping her along that she didn't even bother to protest.

"A happy, loving couple, how touching." Brent was standing looking down at her as Eric disappeared through the door, and Kessie returned his gaze without flinching.

"You must believe what you wish," Kessie said flatly. "I'm not trying to explain any more. I feel I've done enough of that."

Brent sat down beside her. "Look, Kessie, I came after you thinking I'd been wrong after all, and then I find Eric kissing you. What do you expect me to make of it?"

"I no longer care what you think about anything." Kessie lifted her chin and stared at him defiantly. She was lying, she did care very much what Brent thought, but she had lowered her pride once too often and it had done her no good at all. Now it seemed all she had left to cling to were the last remnants of her self-respect.

Brent leaned closer to her, his eyes uncomfortably shrewd. It was as though he could look into her very thoughts.

"I'm trying to understand," he said, "but you are making it very difficult, I don't like to think of you as the sort of woman who leaps into marriage simply for security."

"Oh, let me be!" Kessie got to her feet and almost ran from the restaurant, tears thick in her eyes although she was determined not to let them overflow.

Brent caught up with her as she went along the corridor towards the lift. He almost propelled her through the open doors, pressing the button so that the doors of the lift closed, effectively shutting them off from any prying eyes.

"Kessie," Brent took her in his arms. "Come here, since you are so free with your kisses."

His mouth was warm and demanding and even though Kessie knew it was with anger he kissed her, not with love, she couldn't help the response that made the blood run quickly through her veins, taking away her strength so that she leaned against Brent, helpless to protest.

The kiss went on and on, her arms wrapped themselves around his broad shoulders and her fingers touched the crisp hair at the nape of his neck where it curled away from his head. She was like a being possessed, she couldn't even try to hide the feelings that flowed through her, she wanted Brent as she'd never wanted any man in her life before.

At last he released her and they stood for a moment simply looking at each other.

The lift stopped and the doors opened and Kessie turned and almost ran from him, shutting herself in her room and flinging herself down on her bed, unable any longer to control the tears that squeezed themselves between her closed lids.

It was an effort later to go downstairs to the office to see what it was Lars wanted. Kessie had dabbed cold water over her reddened eyelids and allowed her hair to hang loosely around her face, hoping to hide her rather wan appearance.

The others were seated in the office already and Kessie made a quick apology, taking a chair in the darkest corner of the room.

"Well." Lars smiled around him, he was certainly looking much fitter than he'd been for some weeks and Kessie was pleased that he had recovered so well.

"I wanted you all to come here," he said, "all of my staff as well as my sons and my dear Kessie here, because I want to tell you my good news." He looked down at Andrea who was seated beside him.

"We are going to married as soon as possible, and I mean exactly what I say, as soon as possible."

There was a murmur of congratulations and Lars held up his hand, smiling.

"Don't cheer too soon," he said. "I want the wedding to take place here at the hotel in a week's time, which will not give anybody a great deal of time for the preparations. But naturally I want the best you can all offer in the way of catering and organisation. Do you think you can do it? Anyone with doubts please let me know at once."

In the general confusion of talk that followed Lars' statement, Kessie caught Brent's eyes. He gave her a half smile and looked away and Kessie bit her lip. Why couldn't he believe her when she'd explained about her so-called engagement to Eric? Was it that he didn't care one way of the other?

The meeting seemed to have split up into small groups of people, each concerned with their own part in the preparations that were to be made. Kessie wondered if she could slip out of the room unobserved. It was so hot in there and she was as ever conscious of Brent's nearness.

"My dear Kessie," Andrea stood at her side. "Why are you looking so miserable? Are you not pleased with my good fortune in marrying such a man as Lars?"

"Of course I'm pleased," Kessie said at once. "I think you'll both be very happy and I'm just deep in thought, that's all."

"Ah, I can well believe that." Andrea's eyes were full of curiosity. "You have your own wedding to think about."

"Well, not just yet," Kessie said quickly, and Andrea sat down beside her, leaning forward.

"Tell me, Kessie, is it really what you want, this marriage to Eric?"

Kessie looked around her, wondering what on earth she could say. She made an effort to smile.

"We are here to talk about your marriage, not mine," she said lightly. "What are you going to wear?"

This was something Andrea was eager to

talk about. She sat back in her chair, her face lit with enthusiasm.

"I'm having a thick cream gown," she said, lifting her heavy dark hair above her head. "My hair will be put up like this and flowers wound in it. I think I will look quite a lovely bride, don't you, Kessie?"

Andrea's conceit had such a tone of innocence in it that Kessie could not help but smile.

"You will be beautiful," she said at once, "and Lars will be so handsome, it will be the wedding of the year."

"Oh, Kessie," Andrea said, "I know I haven't much intelligence and I won't be much help to Lars in his business, but I will try hard to make him proud of me, I love him so much."

Kessie felt a lump come to her throat. She envied Andrea, that she had found happiness with the man she loved, which was something never likely to come Kessie's way as things were now.

"Right." Lars' voice carried across the room, "I think I can safely leave all the arrangements to my staff and I am grateful to you all, thank you."

Kessie was one of the first to leave the room. She hurried along the corridor and made her way to the pool where there were comparatively few people. She sank down on to one of the sunbeds and closed her eyes, trying to blot out the vision of Brent's sardonic smile and the coldness in his grey eyes.

Her unhappiness had been highlighted by the joy in Andrea's face when she'd talked about Lars, and now she felt as though she simply could not cope with the situation at all.

"Kessie." Brent stood looking down at her and when she opened her eyes she could have thought for a moment that there was tenderness in his expression.

"Yes?" she sat up, flattening the creases from her skirt.

"You can't go through with it, can you?" He crouched down beside her, his face close to hers. She pretended not to understand him.

"Go through with what?" She avoided his eyes, there was too much he might read in hers.

"This silly engagement." He took her fingers in his and she drew a sharp breath.

"But you acted as though you thought it was what I wanted," she said, trying to control the trembling in her voice.

"I've been watching you," he said. "You seem unhappy." He tipped her face up and smiled down at her. "You don't love Eric, do you?"

There was the sound of footsteps beside her and Kessie saw a frown come to Brent's face as he got to his feet.

"I don't think Kessie has to answer to you for anything," Eric moved into Kessie's line of vision, his face tight with anger.

"You aren't listening to him, are you?" he said to Kessie. "He is no good, he won't offer you an honourable marriage as I've done."

Kessie looked up at Brent, waiting for him to speak, but he seemed amused rather than angry at Eric's outburst.

"I don't think Kessie wants to marry you, Eric," he said casually. "She doesn't exactly seem overjoyed at the prospect."

Eric went white. "You are a fine one to make comparisons in other people's feelings," he said. "Have you told Kessie about the Danton?"

"No, is there any reason why I should?" Brent asked, almost casually.

"I think she might like to know that you were the one to buy it from father although you tried to keep your identity a secret at the sale."

"So what?" Brent said. "I have the right to buy any property I wish. It's my own money I'm using, not yours, you don't have any of your own."

"I don't think Kessie cares about that," Eric said. "I have a higher opinion of her feelings that you seem to have."

"Wait!" Kessie said and the two men looked at her.

"Brent, is this true, have you bought the Danton?" she said.

He nodded. "Yes, it's true. Why, does the

prospect bother you, you didn't mind selling it to Father."

"It bothers me," Kessie said, "because you told me the hotel was losing money. You made me feel guilty because Lars had thrown good money away on it. I felt I'd almost ruined him and now you have bought it. Why? What's going on?"

"Can't you see?" Eric broke in. "He wanted the hotel for himself all along the line. He told you all those lies as he told them to my father so that the hotel would fall into his hands whenever he wanted it."

"That's absurd," Brent said easily. "The hotel was losing money."

"Then why did you bid for it?" Kessie asked slowly. "I fully intended to buy it back from Lars but you outbid me. Though I never imagined for one minute it was you who had bought the hotel. Why did you?"

"That's my business," Brent said calmly. "I don't wish to explain my actions at this moment."

"Not at any moment," Eric said sneeringly. Kessie looked at him, not knowing which brother she despised more. She pulled off the engagement ring and handed it to Eric.

"Here," she said, "I don't intend to marry you and I never did, and if you choose to tell your father about it that's your decision, not mine."

"But Kessie," Eric began, "don't act so hastily. Surely you can see that Brent is not worthy of you." He tried to take her hand but Kessie pulled away from him in disgust.

"Leave me alone, can't you!" she said. "I never want to see either of you again, and once this wedding is over I'm leaving Norway for good."

She rushed out of the room, unaware of the curious eyes of the other people around the pool, and hurried towards her room, running up the stairs unable to wait for the lift. She wanted to put as much distance as she could between Brent and herself. Eric she didn't care about, she had never cared about him, but now it seemed that Brent had fooled her and fooled his father too, probably, by saying the Danton was a failing concern. Why, oh, why had he said such a thing? It just didn't make sense.

She meant what she had said to Eric, once Lars and Andrea were married there would be nothing to keep her here, nothing at all.

The wedding day dawned bright and clear but with a cold wintery wind blowing in spite its being only autumn.

"Thank goodness it's so warm in here," Andrea said, pulling her long skirt around her feet, looking beautiful and bridal in her cream gown. "Here, Kessie, can you arrange the hemline for me?" she asked anxiously. "It seems to be falling lower in the back than the front."

"No, it's fine now," Kessie assured her, "it was just rucked up a little, that's all."

"Oh, Kessie," Andrea said, "I'm so nervous and excited. Will we be happy, do you think?"

"Of course you will," Kessie said, making the effort to smile. "Anyone could tell that you and Lars were made for each other."

A strong easterly wind rattled the windows, whipping the trees outside into a frenzy. Kessie shivered as though an icy hand had touched her.

"Oh, it will be wonderful to get away from here for some real sunshine," Andrea said. "I'm so pleased that Lars agreed to take me to Italy for our honeymoon."

"You're very lucky," Kessie agreed. "I wouldn't mind some warm climate myself as this moment."

She glanced at her watch. "I think it's about time we went downstairs now, don't you?" She smiled reassuringly at Andrea. "You look really lovely, don't worry."

Andrea bent forward and kissed Kessie's cheeks. "I'm so glad you're here," she said. "I've grown quite fond of you over these last months, and I think you're the nearest thing to a family I've got."

"I'd hug you if I wasn't afraid of spoiling your hair. Come on, the ceremony will be starting in a couple of minutes," Kessie said quickly, touched more than she cared to say by Andrea's words.

Everything went beautifully, the simple ceremony quickly over, and then Lars, with

Andrea on his arm, walked down the strip of red carpet towards the stairway.

"Catch, Kessie!" Andrea said, turning and throwing her bouquet, and instinctively, Kessie held out her hands and caught it neatly.

"You will be the next one married!" Andrea laughed jubilantly, and hurried away up the stairs to change into her travelling clothes.

There was the clink of champagne glasses and the rise and fall of voices all round Kessie but she could think of nothing but Andrea's words. They turned round and round in her mind, as though taunting her, and she swallowed hard, trying to pull herself together.

Later, Lars and Andrea came down to give their farewells and suddenly Lars picked up Kessie's hand.

"My dear!" he said in concern. "Where is your ring, you're not wearing it."

"I'm sorry, Lars," Kessie said. "I didn't want to mention it just now but Eric and I have decided we won't be getting married after all."

"This is impossible!" Lars said, his face full of concern. "Have you had a silly lover's tiff? If so, make it up, my dear. I so much want you as part of my family."

"Don't you worry about me," Kessie said. "You just enjoy yourselves and come back brown and happy."

"Oh, but Kessie." Andrea took her arm, "Lars and I want you to be happy. Come on, if it's just a simple misunderstanding between you and Eric, make it up before we go."

Kessie bit her lip, trying to think of something to say that would persuade the couple that she was all right.

"I'll tell you what," she said at last. "I'll promise to talk things over with Eric. There, does that suit you?"

Andrea smiled. "I'm sure everything's going to be all right for you," she said. "I want everyone to be as happy as I am at this moment."

"That's asking a great deal." Kessie pushed at Andrea's shoulder gently. "Now, go on, both of you, enjoy yourselves and leave us to sort out our own problems."

Andrea sighed and she and Lars would have moved away except that Eric stepped forward.

"Just a minute," he said, and Kessie took a deep breath. She had no idea what Eric was going to say but instinctively she knew it meant trouble.

"Please Eric," she said impulsively. "Let your father and Andrea get away. It is their wedding day after all and they don't want to have to listen to our petty little worries."

Eric was determined to be heard, his eyes were sharp as they stared down at Kessie and she knew nothing she could say would stop his outburst.

"You know the real reason that Kessie and I quarrelled, don't you, Father?" he said in a harsh voice, and Lars looked at him quickly.

"I don't believe I do," he said quietly, "but I'm sure you're going to tell me, Eric."

"It's because Brent went behind all our backs and bought the Danton Hotel. Kessie thinks we're all tarred with the same brush, all cheats and liars like my precious brother." He paused, and as his words were met by silence, he went on.

"Oh, yes, Kessie has no time for any of us now. But tell her, Father, you knew nothing of this, did you?"

Kessie spoke quickly. "That's not true!" she said looking earnestly at Lars. "I'm disappointed that Brent outbid me for the hotel but I don't hold any grudges, not against anyone. Good luck to Brent. Perhaps he can make a success of it, I certainly hope so."

She put her hand on Lars arm. "Please don't let any of this worry you, just go away and forget all about it."

Lars smiled. "Don't you worry about me, my dear, and as to the Danton Hotel, I knew what Brent's intentions were long ago."

Eric gave an exclamation of surprise. "You knew and didn't stop him?"

"On the contrary," Lars said coolly, "I helped him raise the capital he required. I have faith in the boy and if anyone can make a go of the place, he can." Lars smiled at Kessie.

"Forgive me for keeping this from you, my dear, I had my reasons and it's up to Brent to tell you all about his plans. Where is Brent anyway?"

"I'm here." Brent stepped out of the shadows and looked grimly at Eric.

"Trust you to make a scene right now. Have you no sense of timing? Do you have to spoil our father's wedding day, just in order to say your little piece?"

"You're a fine one to talk!" Eric said, "You are forever acting like you were a saint or something, and now I find you've persuaded Father to back you financially so that you can get away, leave all your responsibilities here, and live it up in London." Eric turned to Kessie, "There, can't you see him in his true colours now?" He caught her hand. "Look, take back the ring, say you'll marry me. I'll be much better to you than Brent would ever be."

"No!" Kessie snatched her hand away. "I don't want to marry you, now or ever, can't you understand that? I just want you all to leave me alone."

Eric's face flushed. "Oh, little miss high and mighty, think you're too good for me, do you?"

Kessie shook her head. "No, now please leave me alone, Eric, I want to go to my room."

He caught her roughly by her shoulders and stared down into her face, his eyes glittering.

"I don't know why I bother with you at all, you're just a cheap little..."

The sentence was never finished because suddenly Brent seized Eric by the collar.

"Take that back!" he said between clench-ed teeth. "No one speaks to Kessie like that, not in my hearing."

"That's right," Eric sneered, "defend her. We all know the reason too, don't we? Didn't I catch you together on the moun-tain, the both of you half undressed?" He looked round at the curious faces trium-phantly.

"Oh, yes, Kessie's good enough to spend

the night with but not good enough for you to marry, isn't that right, Brent?"

With a cry, Kessie turned away and ran along the empty corridor to her room. Her face burned with anger. Whatever Eric's faults might be, he'd just hit the nail on the head. Brent didn't think she was good enough to marry and that was an end to it.

Hastily, she opened the drawer and began to pack. The sooner she was away from the hotel Sornefjord and away from Brent, the better she would feel.

TEN

Nothing could shake Kessie's determination to leave the hotel and even as she stood in the foyer, her suitcase at her side, Lars almost pleaded with her to change her mind.

"The hotel needs you," he said, "and in any case there's no transport down to the valley. I'm taking the helicopter, remember, and now the weather seems to be getting worse, you can't risk riding down on horseback."

"I'll have to risk it," Kessie said, staring round her, taking in the details of the hotel for the last time. "I'm not staying here now and that's final, Lars. I don't want you to worry about it but on the other hand I'm not changing my mind, either."

"Won't you even talk to Brent about your decision?" Lars asked. "He might be able to change your mind."

"No way!" Kessie said sharply. How could she say that Brent was the main reason for her leaving? She would get away from him once and for all, and when she returned to London, she would make a new life for herself and forget Brent and all the rest of the Tolkelarson family too, if it came to that.

Lars sighed. "Very well, then you must come with Andrea and me in the helicopter." He glanced at his watch. "We must leave soon or we'll miss our connection."

Kessie looked at him contritely. "I'm sorry," she said. "I know I'm the reason you've delayed your take-off but if I may come with you, Lars, I'll be very grateful."

Brent came into the foyer, his eyes on Kessie's suitcase. She glanced away from him, disturbed as ever by his lean good looks and by the challenging way he stood beside her.

"You're not really leaving, Kessie?" he

asked, and even now, she wasn't sure if she detected a hint of amusement in his voice.

"Yes, I'm leaving," she said. "Lars has told me I can go with him in the helicopter."

"You're not going up in that damned machine again, Father?" Brent said quickly. "I understood you were having a pilot from the valley to take you."

"I was," Lars said flatly, "but he hasn't turned up so unless I fly the thing myself, Andrea and I are going to miss our honeymoon."

He moved towards the door and Kessie swallowed hard as Brent forestalled her when she bent to pick up her case.

"I'll take that for you," he said and for a brief instant his fingers touched hers. She drew her hand away sharply and followed Lars outside into the crisp coldness of the air, trying to stop the rush of emotions that made her long to fling herself into Brent's arms.

"I don't like this," Brent said as he helped her into the helicopter. "I'm sure Father shouldn't be flying, he's not fit enough, especially in such cold weather conditions."

Kessie looked through him, it was the only way she could keep herself from breaking down into tears of anger and frustration that he was so calmly letting her go out of his life.

Nevertheless, his words penetrated her misery and she glanced anxiously at Lars. He was smiling and seemed as fit as he'd ever been.

" 'Bye everyone!" Andrea was leaning out waving her hand frantically, and then the helicopter lifted smoothly off the ground and the hotel gradually appeared to grow smaller. The people standing in the snow outside were like small, moving dots.

"Are you sure you want to go now Kessie?" Lars shouted over the roar of the rotor blades.

"Yes, I'm sure," Kessie shouted back, and settled back into her seat, closing her eyes, determined not to look down again. What was past couldn't be altered but once she was among her own sort in the busy whirl of London, she would quickly forget Brent.

Then she could begin to live a life with some order in it again.

She must have dozed because suddenly a strange noise made her come sharply awake.

"What's wrong?" she asked, and Lars glanced at her over his shoulder.

"I'm not sure, the engine seems to be faltering. It's nothing to worry about, I can easily land if the going gets too tough."

He did some things with the controls, and at his side Andrea, her eyes wide, watched him, her fur coat clutched round her as though for protection.

"Brent was right," she said quickly. "We should never have allowed you to fly, not in these weather conditions."

"I'm perfectly all right, my dear," Lars said, but there was an edge of strain to his voice that Kessie couldn't fail to notice.

"Look," she said, pointing downwards, "there's a flat place there, perhaps it would be better if we landed, then you could use the radio to call for help."

"You could be right, Kessie," Lars agreed. "There seems to be quite a gale blowing up and if it snows I won't be able to see a thing. Damn!" He said softly, "I wish I'd had more experience of flying this thing."

He brought the machine lower just as a burst of snow seemed to come from no-where, blanketing the surrounding snowy mountainside so effectively that one part looked exactly like another.

There was a silence for a moment and then Kessie leaned forward, tapping Lars on the shoulder.

"What if we open the door," she said, "then I could hang out and tell you when there was a safe piece of ground on which you could land."

Lars shook his head. "No, it's too danger-ous, I couldn't let you take such a risk."

He flew the machine in silence for a few seconds and then the rotor blades seemed almost to stop. The helicopter surged down-wards while Lars frantically altered the con-trols.

Andrea was hunched in her seat, her face white, and Kessie felt sorry for her.

"What if we abandon our luggage?" she

asked suddenly. "That might help."

Lars smiled at her. "I don't think it would do much good, I think the blades are icing up but go ahead if it makes you feel any better."

The activity seemed to bring Andrea alive and she pushed out cases with a determination that brought colour to her cheeks.

"I think Kessie's ideas are sensible ones," she said to Lars. "Why don't you allow her to look out for a place for us to land? It might be our only chance."

Lars shrugged. "I don't think I have any alternative. All right, Kessie, get right down on the floor and try to find a suitable place, but for heaven's sake, hold on tight."

Kessie scrambled from her seat and the ice cold wind struck her in the face as she leaned over the floor of the helicopter. The ground swung away alarmingly beneath her and for a moment, her eyes were almost blinded by snow.

"Try to get a little lower," she shouted, and Lars carefully manoeuvred until they were nearer the ground. "Lower still!" Kessie said, the wind catching her words and taking them away.

So suddenly that she didn't know what happened the helicopter swung sideways and she was tipped out of the cockpit, hurtling downwards towards the snowy mountain, the wind taking the breath from her lungs.

She heard herself scream and then she landed in a bed of cold softness that cushioned her body in white while a few feet away stood the jagged point of a rock.

She lay still for a moment, shivering, knowing only that she was lucky to be alive. Then below her somewhere, she heard an ominous crunching sound that raked the air and then there was nothing but the falling snow and a deathly silence.

She forced herself to struggle out of the drift of snow that had saved her life. She ached as though she were bruised all over but at least there were no bones broken.

She leaned forward against the wind, making an effort to struggle downwards. She must try to find Lars and Andrea, they had the radio and would call for help, but she knew if she didn't find warmth and shelter, she wouldn't last until the rescue party could be sent out.

She walked for what seemed hours, losing all sense of direction. Once or twice she made an effort to call out but the cold seared into her lungs, making breathing difficult, and eventually she fell silent, hardly conscious as she struggled onwards.

Once, she sank down into the snow, her legs failing to support her, and she was tempted by an overwhelming tiredness to lie where she had fallen.

She climbed to her knees and forced herself into an upright position. She knew it would be sure death to give in to her feelings of langour.

She was walking almost blind when she bumped into something. At first she thought hopefully that it was the helicopter but her hand encountered the rough surface of a door. It was the hut where she and Brent had spent the night when she had first come to Norway.

"Please open," she murmured, leaning all her weight against the door. Her strength had almost gone and it took all the determination she could muster to keep pushing against the unyielding surface.

At last when she was almost on the point of giving up, the door swung in with a creak of breaking ice and Kessie found herself out of the biting wind. She pushed the door shut and crawled forward. Her eyes were heavy and though she knew that she should try to light a fire, or at least cover herself with one of the blankets that lay in the corner, she could no longer resist the urge to sleep.

When she opened her eyes again, she thought she must be dreaming. A bright fire glowed beside her so that she could feel its welcome warmth on her face. She was wrapped like a cocoon in a blanket, and when she raised her eyes from the leaping flames of the fire, she saw Brent sitting on the other side of it, grinning at her.

"How did you find me?" she asked. Then her memory of what happened returned.

"Andrea and Lars, are they all right?"

"Hey, hold on!" Brent raised his hand in protest. "One question at a time please." He moved nearer to her and smoothed the hair back from her face.

"They're both fine. Thanks to the radio message that Father was able to send out we found his position easily enough. You proved the difficulty as usual." His smile took all the sting out of his words. "Fortunately, it didn't snow for very long and I was able to pick up your trail."

Kessie tried to sit up. "I suppose we'll be getting to the hotel now before nightfall."

Brent grinned again. "Too late, it's dark already, I'm afraid we're going to have to stay the night again."

Kessie looked away from the unexpected tenderness in his eyes. Her heart was beating so fast it was a wonder Brent couldn't hear it.

"Kessie." He tipped her face up and stared down into her eyes. "Do I have to spell my feelings out to you? I love you, silly little fool."

His lips touched hers and she lay, weak and unresisting, in his arms wondering if she were just a little delirious.

"Kessie, when I bought the Danton, it was with the express idea of taking you back there, as my wife."

He kissed her again, this time more searchingly, and Kessie struggled free of the folds of the blanket so that she could put her arms around him and hold him close.

"I love you," Brent said. "Do I have to give you more proof?"

"Yes, Brent," Kessie said with a sigh. "Give me more proof," and willingly he covered her mouth with his once more.